The Proving Years

The Proving Years

BY

CATEAU De LEEUW

ILLUSTRATED BY LEONARD VOSBURGH

THOMAS NELSON & SONS

Edinburgh   NEW YORK   *Toronto*

by Cateau De Leeuw

THE TURN IN THE ROAD

FEAR IN THE FOREST

ONE WEEK OF DANGER

WHERE VALOR LIES

WILLIAM TYNDALE, MARTYR FOR THE BIBLE

FOREWORD

Very little has been written about the army which General Harrison led in the War of 1812, or the fighting in which it took a part. There have been accounts of the New York campaign, the burning of Washington, the gallant sea-fighting, the famous battle of New Orleans, but too often the hardships and suffering of the Army of the Northwest have been forgotten.

Harrison was a wise general, but he was hampered in various ways. He did not always have competent officers, he was usually short of supplies and men. The weather, the swamps, and the lack of decent roads (or any roads at all) nearly proved disastrous several times.

He went to Ohio to take command after the tragic surrenders of Detroit, Dearborn, and Michilimackinac. There was panic among the settlers of the northern country, and there was good reason for the panic. The citizens of less threatened states could not know the fear which the Shawnee chief Tecumseh and his Indians inspired.

Tecumseh was a wise general, too, but *he* was hampered by the unruly nature of the tribesmen he was trying to weld into a single fighting force and by his allies, the British, who were less clever in warfare and less generous than he to their captives.

5

These two wise generals were pitted against one another for the second time. Harrison had won a victory over Tecumseh at Tippecanoe in 1811, but it had been a costly one which had enhanced the reputation of the Shawnee chief as much as it had brought fame to his American foe.

Harrison dared not move against Tecumseh and the British until he had enough men distributed across a wide front to guard his rear when he advanced. He could not invade Canada or go to the relief of Detroit until the British navy on Lake Erie had been defeated.

The story of Commander Perry's remarkable feat in building a navy, arming it, and manning it is a glorious one, and it has been told many times. Once the British navy on the lake was out of the picture, Harrison was free to go ahead, and the invasion of Canada and the triumphant battle of the Thames followed rapidly.

There were regulars in Harrison's army, but most of his men belonged to the militia—ordinary citizens with the stubborn individualism of pioneers. They did not wear smart uniforms and towering leather shakos. Most of them were farmers or artisans, and they wore the clothing that they wore at home or at work, clothing which often proved inadequate during the icy winter campaign. They usually owned their rifles and knew how to use them, but they did not present a very handsome appearance on parade.

Unwilling to accept discipline, unruly under command, the militiamen admired Harrison enough to accept him as their general, and to fight when they had to. Without them, he could never have succeeded, for the regular army at that time was incredibly small.

Jason and his brother Eph, his friend Andy and Eph's friend Abner, are typical of the militiamen who served under Harrison. There were men like Jonathan Dodge, too. And there were brave spies like James Dineen. This is their story, and the story of all those who fought under General Harrison in the years which proved to the world that these United States had become a nation to be reckoned with.

C. De L.

The Proving Years

CHAPTER 1

Jason and Eph stood awkwardly at the head of the lane before Nan's house, wishing that the family farewells were over. Their brother Robert, their married sisters Nan and Tabitha, however, were unwilling to let them go.

Nan caught at Jason's arm as he turned away. "Wait!" she said. "I've made you a shirt to take along."

"I got a shirt from home," Jason said, heaving a short sigh of impatience. "But thanks all the same," he added belatedly.

"You'll thank me when winter comes," his sister said with an air of complacency. "If you call that thing you're wearing a shirt—all rags and patches—well, I don't know what's to become of the two of you."

Eph grinned. "We'll make out all right. Always have."

"I suppose they will," Tabitha said. "The two of them are more Indian than white, I do believe. Not like the rest of the family at all."

Her brood of three clung to her muslin skirts. Her husband, hair slicked into a fashionable cowlick, stood in the background. Jason thought that Tabitha had managed to forget her pioneer childhood pretty quickly.

"The rest of the family fought Injuns," Eph said

11

mildly. "Had to, when they first come out. Come to think of it, you were pretty good with a rifle yourself, Tabby."

"I never was!" she cried indignantly. The others, reminded of their earlier days, had to laugh. Tabitha, more than any of them, had taken to city life, once she had married the son of a prosperous Cincinnati lawyer.

Jason's brother Robert had stood silent for some time. Now he spoke. "If you should meet a man by the name of Brinkley—Tom Brinkley—tell him I've not forgot."

"Where did you know him?" Tabitha asked.

"When I marched with Harrison at Tippecanoe," Robert answered.

"What did he do? Save your life?" That was Nan, the romantic one.

"Borrowed money," Robert said laconically, and Eph chuckled.

"I'll tell him. But likely I'll spend the money if I collect it from him."

Jason stood first on one foot and then on the other. He was anxious to get going. He and Eph had a way to go before nightfall if they were to join the militia assembling at Franklinton. Not that *he* was joining, he added, honest even with himself, for he was too young. They didn't take lads of fourteen in the militia, though he couldn't see why not. But Eph was joining, and he was sure that a place would be found where Jason could be useful, too.

Nan's two children were racing about the garden, whooping like a couple of little Indians. Now they came panting toward the group of older folk. "Take me along!" "Woo-woo-woo! I'm an Injun!" Eph pretended to be afraid, and dodged behind a tree, while Jason fingered the knife at his belt with a scared expression on his face.

"Don't clown!" Tabitha said sternly, and both of her brothers straightened up sheepishly. It had been a happy day for them when Tabitha had married and gone to live in town.

"Well, we'll be going," Eph said. "Write when you kin. I'll let you know where we're stationed."

As they went down the lane they could hear Tabitha saying, in an aggrieved voice, "I always knew Jason would grow up to be a little savage. We should never have left him to be reared by Eph when Ma and Pa died."

Robert, as if to drown out anything more she might say, called out, "Give it to the British, lads! You show them that America has only one traitor like Hull!"

Eph chuckled. "The two of us don't make much of an army, do we? But he's right, at that. It's up to us men from Ohio to wipe out Hull's surrender."

Jason nodded; neither he nor his brother was talkative. But his thoughts were busy.

There had been talk of war with England for a long time before this autumn of 1812. Talk of impressed seamen, of seized ships. But these things did not mean too much to the people of Ohio. They had another concern, and a grave one, for their frontier was the bulwark against invasion from Canada. Even more important, it was the first line of defense against the Indians led by Tecumseh, who was trying to form the different tribes of his people into a powerful confederation. Hull's futile efforts against the British, followed by his cowardly surrender of Detroit, had roused the men of the Old Northwest.

Jason's parents had come to the Ohio country when neighbors sometimes lived miles away. They had cut a farm out of the forest, had fought for every inch of their land. Nan and Robert could remember those early days well, and there was something in their steady gaze, their firm handclasp, that spoke of self-reliance gained the hard way.

Tabby had been born here, but by the time she was in her teens the farm was surrounded by other farms, and the Indian menace had disappeared from their part of the state. Eph, Jason decided, must be something like their pa whom he scarcely remembered for Jason was the youngest of all the Potter children. There had been four young ones between himself and Eph, but they had all died early.

Eph said, almost as if he had been thinking the same thoughts, "Queer, ain't it, how different folks in the same family can be?"

"I'm glad we're to fight under Gen'l Harrison."

"Like you and Tabby?" Jason asked.

"Yes, and like Tabby and Nan."

A quarter of a mile farther on, he said, "Sometimes I'm not sure it was a good thing to keep you with me when you were so little."

"Why, Eph!" Jason was startled. "You know I wanted to stay with you."

"But mebbe you shouldn't have. I know my own strengths and my own failin's. I know I'll never be a farmer or a tradesman. I'll never farm more than enough to keep myself in victuals. And I've raised you the same way. Mebbe if I hadn't, you'd be headed some other way."

It was a surprising speech for Eph to have made, and Jason realized that the seriousness of the occasion had prompted it. He could not imagine wanting to be different from Eph—knowing the ways of the woods, a hunter by choice, a farmer by necessity.

He said, "When the war's over, do you think we might settle farther north? Where the game's not so scarce?"

"Might." Eph had relapsed into his habitual chariness of words.

Jason said, "I'm glad we're to fight under Gen'l Harrison. I haven't heard much good of that Winchester."

"Nobody has."

"It's good we waited to get rid of the farm. It's taken all this time for Harrison's commission to come in."

They walked in silence for a while, the golden air

of October sifting through the tree branches. Suddenly Eph stopped and Jason, long trained in a woodsman's ways, stopped instantly beside him. Then Eph resumed his long stride and Jason, his eyes fixed on the man who had appeared in the road ahead of them, said softly, "Think he's headin' our way?"

Eph did not answer, but the man, hearing them come, stopped to wait for them.

"Howdy, friends," he said with an easy smile, shifting his rifle to his left arm. "My name's Abner Bowen, and I'm for Franklinton to join the militia."

"We are, too," Jason said quickly, and then could have bitten his tongue, for Eph's side-glance rebuked him.

"Fine, fine. Be glad to have your company. Three's better'n one any day, and though they say the Injuns hereabouts are all friendly, I'm not one to trust *any* of the critters."

"There are good and bad ones, same as any people," Eph said. Jason noticed that he had not committed them to the company of the stranger.

"O' *course* there are. It's just unfortunate, you might say, that I've only met the bad ones so far. And my folks before me. Three scalpin's in my family in one generation."

All the time they were talking, Eph and Abner Bowen had been walking steadily, Jason a step or two behind them. He would have liked to ask the stranger where he came from, what outfit he was going to join, and whether he had ever fought any Indians himself, but he kept silent. He wasn't going to risk another of those looks from Eph.

The other man, sensing that Eph was not as friendly as he might have been, walked in silence, too. Finally he said, "I'm joining up account of that traitor Hull. What got into him to surrender Detroit when there was no need to? A shame and a disgrace, that was! I hope he gits his deserts."

"So do all decent men." Eph's voice was slightly warmer now.

"And as for Cap'n Heald—he was no traitor, but he must ha' been a real fool to hand over Fort Dearborn to the Injuns, give 'em powder and flour, to boot, and then walk out'n the place with hundreds of 'em just waitin' for him!"

"He was only obeyin' orders," Eph said mildly.

"Orders! Arrgh!" Bowen growled. "Orders like that should never be obeyed."

"Aye," Eph said, "I think I'm with you there. But we've been raised on the frontier where a man has to do his own thinkin'."

"If he don't, he won't have no hair to his head," Abner Bowen laughed, his good humor restored. "But I'll tell you one thing—I'm joinin' the militia, but I ain't handin' over my scalp to some whoopin' Injun, just because an officer tells me to."

Jason grinned. There had been tales of unruly militia ever since the war began, and even before. The men who came from their farms or their workbenches to fight the British and the Indians were an independent breed. They had no uniforms, their faces seldom knew a razor, their rifles were their own, and their terms of enlistment were short. Once they had elected their own officers, they were as apt as not to disobey them if they felt commands were unfair.

He remembered stories of near and outright mutiny. Why, when General Harrison had marched to the relief of Fort Wayne only last month, the men under General Winchester had been all set to walk out and go home, because they felt no confidence in their commander. They wanted to serve under Harrison or no one, and it had taken all of Harrison's eloquence to persuade them to stay under Winchester.

Now that General Harrison had finally been given command over the whole of the Northwest, there was less muttering in the ranks. But there was still friction and distrust between the men of the regular army and those of the militia. There always would be, Jason supposed. Their very natures were different.

He roused from his thoughts when he heard Bowen say, "How about the lad? He goin' to stay with friends while you're gone?" A jerk of his head toward the rear told that he was talking about Jason.

Eph did not answer at once. Then he said slowly,

"Jason's a good hunter and woodsman. One of the best.
I think there'll be a place for someone like him."

"Mmmm. Mebbe." Bowen turned and scrutinized
Jason's tall, rangy body, the easy way he carried his
rifle, the well-worn knife at his belt, his steady eyes and
firm jaw. "Too bad he don't shave yet—he could pass for
older. . . . But there's always jobs to be done and paid
for in an army."

What jobs? Jason wondered. Waiter to an officer?
Hunter of game? Messenger? Without any outward expression of the excitement within him, he wondered
what the near future held for him.

CHAPTER 2

J̇ASON blew on his cold hands. He turned to his new friend, whose nose was even redder than his, and said, "I doubt we'll git into Canada this winter."

Andy shivered. "Should ha' done it this fall, but I reckon we couldn't."

"Then why do we have to stay up north here and freeze?" Jonathan Dodge whined. "Men are slippin' out between the pickets every night now—not waitin' for their enlistment to be up. They might as well be comfortable at their own firesides, say I."

Jason was thoughtful. "I know Gen'l Harrison *wanted* to attack Canada last fall, but Eph says it just couldn't be done. If he had gathered all his men together in one place so's to do it, the Injuns could ha' slipped around to the rear. He has to cover the whole northwest country, and that means he hasn't enough men to invade."

"He had nigh on ten thousand!" Jonathan cried indignantly. "That was enough to whup the hull British nation!"

"If they were from Ohio," Andy agreed, and a chorus of voices from behind them chimed in. "From Indiana, you mean!" "From Kentuck!"

They laughed a little, then sobered again. It was too cold to be merry.

"Well, Eph says, too, there wasn't enough supplies for an advance—too many supply trains bogged down in the mire, and too few roads, and them bad ones."

"And there's the artillery," somebody called out. "That makes for slow travelin'."

"Just the same, the longer we wait, the bigger the British army'll be. With the ice on Lake Erie, we could be across to Canady and back before they even knew we were comin'."

"Hmp! That goes for them, too. We better double our sentries when there's a big freeze."

"We've got it right now!"

Jason smiled to himself. There were complaints, and it surely was raw and cold, but he liked most of the men he had met since he and Eph had joined up. Since Eph had joined up, he corrected himself. But he felt as if he, too, belonged to the militia.

Sure enough, there had been plenty for him to do. With rations often scarce, the game he was able to bring in helped to feed the hungry soldiers, and when he wasn't out hunting he was helping around the stables. He had always been successful in treating sick animals, and with so many of them there were always a few ailing ones for him to physic.

"Potter! Jason Potter!" came in a stentorian bellow

from behind the barracks where they were crouched out of the wind.

"That's Sergeant Hawkes," Andy whispered. "What you done?"

Jason couldn't think of any wrongdoing—at least during the past few days—but he rose to his feet. "I'd better find out."

"Want me to go along?"

"No, I don't mind him," Jason said with more than a touch of bravado. Grown men sometimes blanched before Sergeant Hawkes' stern gaze and colorful language.

Jason rounded the corner of the building. "Want me, sir?" he said, sketching a half-salute before the lanky sergeant.

"This little lady's horse went lame on the way here," Hawkes said gruffly, but with the best grace he could muster. "I told her you had a way with critters."

Only then did Jason look up at the rider. His eyes had been admiring the grace and temper of the mare before him. Smooth chestnut coat, with only one small, crescent-shaped white mark on her forehead. A beauty! Good lines and plenty of spirit, even though she was mired from the day's ride.

The girl perched on the saddle could have been described in the same way. She was small and dainty, with large gray eyes and soft, light brown hair. She, too, had plenty of spirit. Jason could tell it just by looking at her, and apparently Sergeant Hawkes could, too, for he was almost deferential in manner as he helped her dismount.

"Here's the lad will take care of your mare," he said. "Jason Potter, his name is. Raised on a farm, but more

at home in the woods, I understand. And there are some say he can actually understand horse-talk."

He guffawed loudly to show that this was meant to be a joke, and the girl laughed, too. She had a merry laugh, unaffected and natural. Not like some ladies Jason had seen. Not even like Tabitha, his sister, who aspired to be a lady in manner and dress.

167

"Miss Vernon is the daughter of Major Vernon," the
sergeant continued, bending a stern gaze upon Jason.
"So see that you cure her horse for her. That's an order."

Jason kept his face straight with an effort. He bent
over to feel the horse's legs, and found a swelling on the
right rear one. "Looks somethin' like a strain," he said
slowly, "but not a bad one."

Lucy Vernon said quickly, "She stumbled in a mud-
hole some distance back, and has been limping ever
since."

"Then that's it," he assured her. "She'll be right again
in no time at all."

Lucy went with him to the stables, although the sergeant tried to dissuade her. "Rough fellows over there,"
he growled. "Not fitt'n' for a lady like you."

"I only want to be sure Diana is comfortable," she
told him with a smile, and he moved aside to let her
pass.

Jason was quick and deft in his bandaging of the
injured leg, and Lucy watched him admiringly. "You *do*
have a way with animals," she conceded. "I can see that
Diana really likes you. She wouldn't let you do this if
she didn't."

He looked up at her from his crouched position beside
the horse. "Animals know right off when you like them,"
he said. "Shows they have more sense than most people."

That was beginning of a real friendship. As the days
went on, and Diana improved, Lucy Vernon's gratitude

became evident. She was almost Jason's age, and there were no others at the fort to whom she could talk easily. Her father was busy with his military duties and had little time to spare for the entertainment of his daughter. Jason sometimes wondered why he had brought her along to this advanced post, where there was danger from a possible Indian attack, and where there were so few comforts for a little lady like Lucy.

"They say her ma died some years back, and she's been livin' with an aunt who's gone back to New England," Eph told him, retailing some of the barracks gossip. "The major wanted to put the lass in a seminary, but she was bound and determined to stay with him, so here she is. I reckon she has a will of her own."

"Aye, she has," Jason said, with a feeling of surprise. He was remembering how easily and surely she had put aside Sergeant Hawkes' effort to keep her out of the stables. And there had been other occasions when she had shown that she could be a very determined young person.

But he worried about her. There were not many women at the post, and those were mostly wives of common soldiers, who did the washing for the officers and men, or who performed other domestic tasks. He thought Lucy must lead a rather lonely life.

Perhaps she did, for she spent more and more of her time with him. She was interested, and truly so, in the life he had led with Eph on the farm. She asked him

THE PROVING YEARS

many questions about himself and his family. And perhaps Jason was a little lonely for folk of his own age,
for he talked to her freely, happy to relive the carefree
days when he and Eph had hunted and fished and
camped out—sometimes for days or weeks—and then had
come back to the old farm to do the chores which would
ensure the minimum of comfort for themselves in the
winter.

He said to her one time, "Days like this, we would
be snug at home by the fire, makin' bullets, or workin'
over a deerskin."

"Had you no animals at all on the farm?" Lucy asked
in wonderment.

"Couldn't have," he said tersely. "Animals take a lot
of care, and several times a day. We couldn't have gone
off on those huntin' trips if we'd had them to tend to."

"Yes, of course, I can see that," she said thoughtfully.
"But then, how did you ever learn to care for animals
and physic them the way you do?"

"Oh, that!" he said with an embarrassed air. "I guess
I've always known how to do that. Just naturally. And
o' course, whenever there was trouble with a neighbor's
critters, they used to call for me to come. People, too,"
he added.

"You mean"—she was wide-eyed—"you mean you
doctored people, too?"

He looked embarrassed. "Well, some. I always tried
to learn as much as I could—there were some folk nearby

that were handy with the sick, and I watched them. Sometimes they let me help them."

"But people—" she began.

"Why not? They're not too much different from farm critters. I mean," he added hastily, "they need the same *kind* of care. A little medicine, some cuttin' sometimes, but not too often, and mostly a—a—" he hesitated, not knowing how to say what he wanted to say—"mostly a sort of feelin' for them."

"I understand," she said, nodding her head. "Sympathetic care."

"That's it," he said quickly, wishing he knew all the words that she knew. "I just couldn't say it right."

"You should be a doctor," she told him, and her voice was serious. "All the learning in the world will not get as good results in doctoring as that kind of ability. I'm sure of it."

He told her something he had never told anyone else. Not even Eph. "I've always wanted to be a doctor. I'm happiest when I'm helpin' sick folk—or animals."

She was silent for so long that he scuffed his moccasin in the snow. Perhaps he shouldn't have told her that. He was on the point of turning away when she said, "If you truly mean that, Jason, then you should prepare for it."

"You mean gather up simples and make a store of them, so's I have 'em handy?"

"No, no!" For the first time, she seemed a little impatient. "I mean in learning. A doctor must know a great deal."

He hung his head. "I know. He has to study, and learn Latin, and read a lot of books . . ." He shrugged. "Well, I kin write my name, but not much more. My sister Nan taught me before she married and left home. And I kin read, but slowly. I'd never—"

"You must practice," she said quickly. "Don't be discouraged, Jason. You have years ahead of you, and if you start now, you can be ready to work with a doctor by the time you're grown."

He snorted. "But I don't *like* learnin'," he protested. "Never did!"

CHAPTER 3

Men were chafing at the inaction. Every time news arrived of Indian depradations—a farm burned, a man scalped and his family captured—there were new desertions. Jason heard mutterings that it was better to be at home defending one's family than waiting for orders to advance against the British.

"What's happened, anyhow?" Abner Bowen said to Eph. "You'd think even Nature was agin this country! Take the Black Swamp between us and Gen'l Winchester. A body'd expect he could cross that easy in a winter cold as this one; but folk that have tried it say it's still too soft most places for travel. And who wants to walk through ice water up to his hips?"

"The Black Swamp was here before this war," Eph said. "That don't mean anything."

"Yes, it does, because they say that Lake Erie's fruz right over near Detroit, and the British kin walk across whenever they want to!"

"Well, while they're walkin' across, why don't *we* walk across to Canada?" Eph asked. "What goes for one, goes for another."

30

"But we can't *git* there account of the swamp!" Abner said. "And if Gen'l Winchester gits into trouble—which he's more'n like to do, from all I've heard of him—he'd better not count on us comin' to his rescue, that's all."

"He's at the rapids of the Maumee now, isn't he?" Jason asked. He always enjoyed listening to Eph and Abner, who were fast friends by this time. They could argue for hours on almost any subject, without either of them losing his temper.

"Aye, so he is, and from what I hear, Gen'l Harrison don't want him there, either. Too far away in case of trouble."

Jason stopped listening for a time while he thought about General Harrison. He had seen him many times, for the general's headquarters this winter had been here at Upper Sandusky. Now that he had seen him he could understand why the men were so fond of him, and why there had been such a popular demand for his command of the armies of the Northwest.

Harrison was lean and energetic. His long narrow face looked longer and narrower framed in the high collar and stock of an officer, and his long nose was set between a pair of kindly eyes. The officers and men of the regular army respected him for his past accomplishments—had he not served his country under General Anthony Wayne in the campaign against the Indians, and was he not the victor at the battle of Tippecanoe?

But he was especially beloved by the men of the mili-

tia—men who had left their homes and had shouldered
guns in order to bring a lasting peace to the newly settled Northwest. They came from Ohio and Indiana and
Kentucky, and there were even some from Pennsylvania
and Virginia. They were willing to march and fight and

die if necessary, but most *unwilling* to suffer army discipline. They were citizens first and soldiers second, and
it took a man like Harrison, who had fought for the
lands he had governed, and who had settled with his
family upon them, to understand their unruliness.

Twice now he had used Jason as a messenger in the
encampment—once to summon an officer with whom he

wished to consult, the other time to take some specifications to one of the engineers. And each time he had bent his kindly gaze upon Jason and had called him by name. This alone was enough to endear him to the boy, for with so many men under him it was astonishing that Harrison could remember a single individual.

The busy scene before Jason's eyes suddenly quickened with excitement. A lathered horse with an exhausted express astride him had just been admitted by the sentries, and was heading toward the house where General Harrison had his headquarters.

Eph and Abner rose to their feet. There were others, like them, who converged upon the house, waiting to hear the news, and guesses were passed from man to man. "The swamp's fruz over!" "The British have landed somewhere!" "Or sunk our navy!" "Nay, it's Massachusetts. They've decided to send a force of militia, after all—two cripples they been tryin' to git rid of!"

That drew a laugh, but one that had an angry note in it, for Massachusetts was so set against this war with England that it had failed to raise the body of militia the President had ordered. Nor was it like to, most men thought. Massachusetts ships spent as much effort in eluding American warships as they did dodging British men-of-war. They were determined to let nothing interfere with their trade with the West Indies.

The laughter broke off as the tired express stumbled out of the house. Men pressed forward eagerly to surround him. They pelted him with questions. Where was he from? What news did he bring? Was it good or bad?

When they learned that he was from General Winchester, more than one mouth was turned down in derision and distaste. And when they learned that Winchester had sent a large detachment of his men northward to defend Frenchtown from the British, there were angry rumblings.

"Frenchtown!" someone said. "But that's only eighteen miles from Malden." Fort Malden, not far from Detroit, was a British stronghold in Canada.

"Well, what could he do? The people at Frenchtown were calling for help. Winchester sent Colonel Lewis, and he's a good man."

Eph said quietly, "Still, it was a fool thing to do. Winchester was far enough away from reinforcements before; now he's really out of reach, and his army is divided. What if—"

"Aye, what if?" Abner broke in furiously. "Those are ifs that any fool but Winchester could answer. We'd best be packin' our traps, for we'll be gittin' orders to foller him."

The words had hardly left his mouth when a stream of messengers began to leave the little house. One of them, spying Jason, and knowing that he had been used for such errands before, called to him. "The general wants you!"

Jason felt his face grow red, for every man turned to stare at him, as if to wonder why *he* should be so important. He raced withindoors, then skidded to a halt as the wiry figure of the general confronted him.

"Ah, Jason, just the lad I want. Tell Major Vernon I want to see him. And when you have done that, best ready yourself for the march. We must be on the road as soon as possible."

Jason was out of the door as soon as Harrison stopped speaking. He did not see Eph or Abner, although they still stood where they had been, so intent was he upon his errand. Rounding a corner, he almost collided with a man, coming just as fast from the opposite direction. But life in the forest had trained him to react quickly, and he dodged sideways. The man caught at his sleeve, bringing him to a halt.

"What's up? Why are you runnin'?"

It was Andy Frazier, Jason's particular friend. But even for him Jason could not stop. "Tell you later," he cried and darted off again.

Major Vernon shared a small house with another officer who had recently arrived, bringing his wife with him. Jason knew that at this hour the major was apt to be sitting at his dispatch case, writing his report. But today he was not there. The little room was empty.

"Why, Jason! What's the matter? If you weren't so brown, I'd say you looked pale!" Lucy laughed at her little joke as she stood in the doorway, but the laughter died at once when she saw the seriousness of his eyes. "What is it?" she asked in a quiet voice.

"Where's your pa? The gen'l wants him—quick!"

"I'll get him." She whirled about and ran out of the house and down the muddy path toward another, smaller house. "Father!" she called. "Father!"

Jason was right on her heels, and when the major came to the door, one of his lieutenants beside him, he gasped out his message. The two men broke into a run, heading across the encampment toward Harrison's quarters.

Lucy sighed. "It *must* be important," she said. "Have you any idea what's happened, Jason?"

"Somethin's happened, that's sure," he answered. "Because the gen'l himself said we should git ready to march. But whatever's happened wasn't good. His eyes were big and he was frownin', and his mouth was pulled in tight like he was mad. I bet it's that Winchester again. The man's a fool!"

Lucy's eyebrows rose a little. "You should not speak that way of your officers," she said primly. "You should show more respect."

Jason glowered at her. "I'm not one to deny respect to them that deserve it," he said with emphasis. "But I don't give it where it don't belong." He spun on his heel and started back toward the barracks.

"Jason!" Lucy called after him, but he did not turn. That's the way regulars were, he thought stormily.

Everything for form, even if it meant denying plain common sense!

By the time he got back to Eph and Abner, the word was all over the camp. Men hurried about their business, readying themselves for a march into the wilderness. Rifles were checked over and inspected with thoroughness, for in the days to come a man's life might well depend upon his gun. Rations were issued, and horses saddled. Wagons were loaded, and teamsters swore and bawled.

The roads in this part of Ohio were so bad, especially in the winter and spring months, that wagon-train horses seldom made more than one or two trips before they were worn out. Pack horses suffered the same fate. Jason hated to see them so badly used.

Cannoneers tugged at the ropes of balky guns, while drivers maneuvered the horses into position before the heavy sleds. There was shouting everywhere. The sudden din was tremendous.

"Ready, Jason?" Eph asked when his younger brother appeared.

"Sure, once I've put on that extra shirt Nan made me take!"

Eph laughed. "Easiest way to carry it this kind of weather," he admitted. "Be sure you have spare moccasins, though. No sense gittin' your feet froze."

Jonathan Dodge came staggering out of the barracks hut so loaded with extra clothing, pans, and blankets that it was hard to see the man beneath the load. "We got to go through that swamp?" he asked in a plaintive voice.

"Sure, unless you want to walk twice as far," Abner said. "But if you take all that truck with you, you'll sink right down to the bottom, and they won't even find a trace of you till next spring."

"They say it's turrible walkin' through that swamp," Jonathan said, "and scarce any place to lie down o' nights. My pa told me that when he was fightin' with Anthony Wayne, there'd be mornin's when a man's queue was fruz fast to the ground and he couldn't git up."

"That's one good reason why men stopped wearin' queues, I reckon," Eph said. "Though the way some of you fellows let your hair grow, it's a wonder it ain't down to your knees!" Eph and Jason always kept their hair short, but many of the militia, especially the men from Kentucky, wore their hair nearly to their shoulders. Eph shaved regularly, too, but a great many of the soldiers wore beards.

Despite everything they said to him, Jonathan insisted on taking most of his belongings with him. "Where'd he git all those things?" Abner wanted to know.

"He has a knowin' hand with the dice," Eph said drily. "He didn't buy them with his pay, that's sure.

Didn't you ever notice that leather purse of his? It's pretty full."

"Well," Jason said with a chuckle, "if anyone has a mind to trail us on the march, he'll be able to do it just follerin' after the things Jonathan's goin' to drop as he tires."

He was right. The troops had gone little more than two miles when Jonathan parted with a pot. "Too heavy," he panted. "Must be made o' lead, not iron!"

By the time they made camp that night, he was too exhausted to do his share of felling trees for pickets and throwing up earthworks for protection. He lay upon his one remaining blanket, too spent to move. Jason went off into the forest as soon as he knew where the encampment was to be, intent on getting some game for supper, and moved so silently through the woods that he surprised one of the rangers, out scouting for possible Indian spies.

"Say, young feller," the man said, "you sure know your way around, don't you? Been brought up a hunter?"

"Aye." Jason was pleased and proud to be congratulated by a man as experienced as James Dineen. He had been watching this man for some time, and following on his trail.

"Lookin' for your supper?"

"I thought I'd bag a couple rabbits if I was lucky."

"Well, if you're as good a shot as you're a stalker, there's some mighty unlucky rabbits hereabouts."

Jason flushed. "I'll go off this way," he said, pointing to the right. "And if I see any Indian sign, I'll let you know."

"Good lad."

They separated, and it was not much later that Jason bagged his "couple rabbits." He hurried back to the camp to cook them for Eph and Abner and Andy and himself. These four had come together over the weeks and formed a small group of their own. Each had his own duties, and Jason's were to hunt the game and cook it. Andy made and tended the fire. Eph and Abner, once their duties were done, usually made a lean-to of some sort as shelter against the cold.

It was while Jason was skinning the rabbits that he had time to think, and his thoughts turned to Lucy. He felt bad about Lucy. He had not learned until just before their departure that her father was to remain at Upper Sandusky and was not to accompany the main body of troops.

When he heard that, Jason had gone at once in search of her, for he wanted to say good-bye. There had been the beginning of a quarrel that morning, and although she had wanted to make peace, he had been too stubborn. Now he felt that if they parted this way, he would have lost a real friend.

There was no sign of her, and he had had to return to the barracks without finding her. But he had left her a token of his friendship. For some time he had been fashioning some blue-jay feathers into a little fan, tying them together with fine linen cord, and fastening them to a handle he had whittled from wood.

Jason was deft with his hands, and the finished fan was something to admire. He wondered if she would know that it came from him.

"What a winter!" Abner said, coming in from his wood-cutting detail. "When you *have* to stay in one spot, and try to keep warm, it's so cold your marrow freezes. And when you have to work hard, the way Eph and I been doin', the weather turns warm on you so's you sweat as if it was summer 'stead of January."

Eph was right behind him. "You worked up a sweat," he said, "because you haven't been doin' anythin' but sit out'n the wind for weeks. Now, take me, I didn't even notice it."

"That's 'cause you got ice water in your veins, not blood," Abner retorted.

Jason spoke up. "Where's Gen'l Harrison? I haven't seen him since he rode down the line early this mornin'."

"He's gone on with Gen'l Perkins from Lower Sandusky," Andy told him. "Likely, the way he travels, he'll make the seventy miles to the Rapids by tomorrow."

"That's a far way," Jason said. "Through the swamp and all."

"So it is," Eph remarked, "but the gen'l is a determined man."

CHAPTER 4

THE columns straggled through the snow and mire. Jason and Eph felt themselves lucky that they traveled light and that they were with the foremost troops. "The fu'ther back you are in an army," Abner said wisely, "the wuss the road gits, from all the tramplin' and the wagons and sleds and cannons that've gone over it ahead of ye. And I'm not even sure you could call this here a road!"

On this evening the van was weary but triumphant. Surely they would reach the Rapids by tomorrow. Andy curled up in his blanket and said sleepily, "Come mornin', I'm goin' to grow me a pair of wings. I'm tired of walkin'!"

The others laughed, but were too weary to joke further, and soon they were asleep. It seemed to Jason that he had scarcely closed an eye when the other one opened to see the first movement in the camp. He grunted a little. War wasn't what he had thought it would be at all. There was little but cold and hunger and marching and swearing. Still, he could not have stayed at home after General Hull's surrender of Detroit.

Eph roused at the same moment. "Today we make it!" were his first words.

Abner sat up, shaking his head, as if to dispel the clouds of sleep, and inquired grumpily, "Make what? Fools of ourselves?"

"Make it to the Rapids. If I have to git in back of this army and push, we're goin' to make it," Eph said firmly.

"Don't bother pushin' the army, just push me," Abner sighed. "Seems like it hadn't ought to be mornin' already. I just laid me down."

There was a stirring everywhere now. Men were gathering up their equipment hurriedly, and munching on their rations. There was an air of dispatch, almost of eagerness, in the ranks.

Now that they were past the Portage River, there was not far to go. Jason thought that Eph would not have any pushing to do, from the spirit of the men. They were on the road as soon as it was light.

Eph and Abner were about mid-column, but an express had no sooner reached the van than the ripple of news spread down toward them. "Word from Gen'l Harrison!"

"Jason, run up a ways and see what it is," Eph said, but he did not need to tell his brother. Jason was already on his way.

He sprinted through the woods alongside the road until he reached the knot of officers clustered together. The heaving, lathered flanks of the messenger's horse identified him at once. Whatever the news he brought, it was good, Jason decided, seeing the pleased smiles on the officers' faces. Yet the commanding general looked a little grim.

Jason poked one of the men nearby. "What news?"

"I dunno. It's from Gen'l Winchester, though."

"Oh, him!"

"Aye, him! Most likely he's done some fool thing again, and we'll have to git him out'n a tight place."

Jason nodded, then waited patiently for the news which would, he knew, soon trickle down to the ranks. In a matter of minutes, it came.

"Colonel Lewis got to Frenchtown?"

"Yep! And he found the British already there—and he licked 'em good and proper!"

"Hooray!"

"Well, he'd better not stay there, now he's licked 'em. Too close to their base," another man chimed in.

But his was a lone voice of caution. There was jubilation everywhere. Jason raced back to his brother to tell him.

"Now we got the redcoats on the run, why don't we go right on into Canada after 'em?" Andy cried. "I hear tell the lake is froze over up that way. No need for boats. We could walk across, and take care of them and Tecumseh and his Injuns at the same time."

"Mebbe that's just what they're expectin' us to do," Abner said quickly. "Likely they'll hole up fust thing, now they've had a taste of what Americans kin do."

Eph said, "We'd be in a pretty exposed position. The reason Harrison didn't want Gen'l Winchester to go to the Rapids in the first place was because he had heard Tecumseh and the Injuns were on Winchester's flank. We have no artillery up here, and practically no supplies. We'd be fools to move until we have those." It was a long speech for Eph.

"Huh! What you afraid of? I know Injuns as well as the next feller, and I know that once they've had a defeat, they scatter. It takes a long time, even for an Injun like Tecumseh, to gather 'em together again, and git 'em riled up to the fightin' point."

"As for supplies, we could live off the country," Andy cried.

"We four could," Eph said. "But most of the men couldn't. The game starts runnin' the minute a big body of men gits near. We'd starve pretty soon without our supply wagons."

"And what do we need cannon for? We got rifles, ain't we?"

"A rifle bullet don't make much of a dent on a fort," Eph said drily.

"Arrgh! If I didn't know you, I'd think you were skeert!" Abner said with disgust. But Jason noticed that neither Abner nor Andy had any more arguments to bring forth, and he decided that Eph had thought things through better than the rest of them.

The news lent speed to the tired men. They moved

ahead much faster now that they had the nourishment
of good tidings. They reached the Rapids that night.

There were few men left there. General Harrison
had sent on General Payne and his men to reinforce
Winchester, and Captain Hart, the inspector general,
bore the good news to Frenchtown of the supporting
troops which were arriving.

"Think they'll send us to Frenchtown, too?" Jason
asked the next morning. "Or do we have to wait for the
rest of the troops?" The others, he knew, were having
a hard time to get through the snow and the half-frozen
swamp.

"I reckon we'll wait," Andy said, "but I wish we
wouldn't."

They settled down to cleaning their rifles, and were
nearly run down by an express who had been passed
by the sentry. Andy shook his head. "I don't see how
the gen'l gits his work done, with all those letters to
read, and reports to write, and all."

"That *is* a lot of his work, I reckon," Jason said. "I
wouldn't want to be an officer."

"No chance anybody's goin' to ask you to be one!"
Andy laughed. The laugh died on his lips, though, as
the encampment sprang to new life. "*Now* what's happened?" he cried, getting to his feet and craning his
neck to see if the furor had originated at Harrison's
headquarters.

Sergeant Hawkes came toward them on the run.

"You, Frazier," he called out to Andy, "fall in with the others. We've orders to march on the double." His hurrying figure disappeared around a corner.

Andy didn't answer. He was gathering his gear together, a serious look upon his face. "I'll bet it's that Winchester," Jason said, loping after him. "Most likely he's got into trouble."

"Most likely we'll git into trouble, too, then," Andy answered with unaccustomed grimness.

The sergeant finished rounding up his men. "We are marching at once," he told them. "Gen'l Harrison's had word that Gen'l Winchester's men were attacked early this mornin' by a large force of Britishers and Injuns."

"They kin beat 'em off," one of the men sang out. "They did it before."

"Not this time," Sergeant Hawkes said. His thin lips had almost vanished, and his mouth was a narrow straight line. "They need help, and need it bad."

"Listen, I got a broke firin'-pin on my rifle," Jonathan Dodge whined. "I can't fight the Injuns with a broke rifle, kin I?"

"You kin git another rifle from the armorer," the sergeant said sarcastically, "but that don't mean you'll be able to fight the Injuns!"

It was obvious that Jonathan was trying to malinger. "Always said he was a shiverin'-livered coward," Abner snorted. "A lot 'o help he'd be in a tight spot! Yet he'd be the fust to yell if he got into trouble."

The men were soon on the road. "Major Gratiot is taking the artillery on sleds over the lake ice," Eph said. "He kin go quicker that way. Not that any way would be quick in this snow."

"Is this Hull's road we're on?" Jason asked.

"That's what I heard tell."

"Well, if it's quicker by the lake, why don't we go that way, too?"

"I don't know. You'd best ask the gen'l that one."

They marched in silence for a while. Jason, young and agile, and a trained woodsman besides, often left them to go through the woods, his eyes and ears alert for signs of the enemy. But there was nothing. Twice he spied James Dineen in the far distance, but he did not think the ranger saw him.

"The way we're goin', we'll pass Payne's men before we know it," Abner said, when they stopped for one of their infrequent rests. "They left yestiddy, but they weren't in the hurry we are."

"The lieutenant's talkin' to somebody up front," Eph said, craning his neck. "Looks like a messenger of some sort from the company ahead."

"Prob'ly askin' for a bullet to chew on."

"What for?"

"He's got a heel blister that hurts him."

The idle joking died away as the lieutenant came toward them, looking purposeful. He stopped in front of Eph and Abner. "I have orders to send on some of my

most active and vigorous men," he said. "I am choosing you, Ephraim Potter, and you, Abner Bowen, from this platoon."

"Hey, I'm as active and vig'rous as they are," Andy said with indignation.

The lieutenant glanced inquiringly at Sergeant Hawkes, who nodded. "Very well, you may go, too,

Frazier. And sergeant, I think you will certainly be needed, as one who is experienced in this sort of warfare."

The sergeant flushed Turkey red with pleasure. "Where we goin'?" he asked.

"I must tell you that we have had dire news," the lieutenant said quietly. "General Harrison, who is well in advance of us, overtook General Payne's troops a while back, and some miles further along the road received word that the French citizens were fleeing from Frenchtown. Some of these fugitives soon arrived in person, with word of the total defeat of General Winchester's army."

There was a stunned silence. "Total defeat!" The words echoed in Jason's head with the sound of doom. "But—but how could that be?" Andy asked the question Jason dared not form into words.

"The attack came early this morning. General Winchester himself was captured. He was encamped along the River Raisin. The men in the town fought valiantly, but"—the lieutenant could scarcely conceal a grimace of disgust—"but General Winchester surrendered anyhow."

"Why, they could ha' won over the British again! They did it before!" Abner growled.

"I think perhaps they could have." The words came slowly, almost reluctantly, from the lieutenant. "But all I know is that those fugitives who have been met say the

British are coming this way." He added, on a bitter note, "And we have been ordered to retreat to the Portage River."

"Retreat!" It was the sergeant. His gruff voice cracked in disbelief.

"Yes, Cotgrove's men have made a forced march to-day with their artillery. They were only fifteen miles from the River Raisin when they got news of the defeat. They couldn't take on the British without us, so they've backtracked pretty far by now. They must be well-nigh exhausted. And there's small use in those of us who took the land road going on unless we have artillery support. No, we have to retreat."

"But then why—" Abner began.

"The general wants some large detachments of men to be sent along different routes to assist, and bring in, whatever fugitives they may find. You men," the lieutenant nodded toward Eph, Abner, Andy, and Sergeant Hawkes, "have been chosen from this platoon."

He started to turn away, but Eph's voice stopped him. "My brother," he said, jerking his head toward Jason, "kin he go along with us?"

The lieutenant frowned. "He does not belong to the army," he said stiffly. "And he's too young."

Jason opened his mouth to protest, but another was before him. "Let the lad go, sir," someone said from the rear of the little group. "I've watched him, and he's as good a woodsman as you're like to find anywhere."

"But—"

"It ain't age but sense that counts in the woods," the voice continued.

"Very well, he may accompany you." The lieutenant sounded a little huffy, as he turned away. But at least Jason had permission to go with Eph on what promised to be a great adventure.

He turned to thank the stranger who had vouched for him, and saw the figure of James Dineen disappearing in the distance.

CHAPTER 5

IT WAS Jason who found the wounded soldier. He had gone ahead of the others, on one of his little scouting trips through the woods, and saw the trail at once. It had been made by someone who stumbled, and there were bloodied patches in the snow where he had fallen.

Jason did not go back to call Eph, but followed the trail for he was sure it was fresh. The huddled figure lay beneath a tree, eyes deep sunk in the sockets and bright with fever. The man half raised himself on one arm, and his thin lips drew back in a snarl of defiance.

"Friend!" Jason cried hurriedly, not knowing whether the fallen soldier would know him for a fellow American. "You from Frenchtown?"

"The British," the man mumbled. "The British are comin'. . . . And the Injuns. Watch out for the Injuns. . . ." But his eyes never left Jason's. He still seemed suspicious.

"You one of Winchester's men?" Jason asked, coming nearer, but cautiously.

"Winchester!" He tried to spit, but could not. His head fell back, and his eyes closed.

54

Jason came up to him. The man had a bullet in his thigh, and one arm was broken. It was a wonder that he had come this far. Quickly, Jason hunted for a strong tree branch that would serve as a splint. With his hatchet, he trimmed it to shape. Then, taking off his hunting shirt, he doffed the shirt Nan had made for him. His hunting knife soon had cut it into strips.

Working quickly, for he wanted to set the arm before the man regained conciousness, Jason braced the limp figure against the tree and, with a quick forceful twist, snapped the two ends of the broken bone together. With the branch to support the arm, and the strips of linen to bind it fast, he was able to do a very neat job within a minimum of time.

The bullet was another matter. That would have to be probed for. And if the man lay here much longer, he would freeze, surely. Jason tried to lift the stranger to his shoulder, but the man was too heavy. The next best thing, then, was to serve as his crutch. But he would have to bring him around first. Jason rubbed snow on the man's face, and was rewarded by seeing the tired eyes open.

"Come, now," he said quickly, when he saw that the lids were going to fall again. "Come with me, and we'll soon git you some proper attention." Half-coaxing, half-ordering, he got the man to his feet. "Now, lean on me and take your weight off'n that leg," he commanded, and started for the road.

Eph and Abner met him before he reached it. They had spied his track as he took off into the woods, and had followed it when he did not return as quickly as usual. "Found one of 'em, did you?" Eph said, approval in his voice, and Jason straightened a little with pride. "That's more'n the rest of us have."

"He'd wandered off the road, what's why," Jason answered. "He was easier to trail than a wounded buck."

"Where'd he git the splint?" Abner wanted to know. "Some surgeon fix him up before he left Frenchtown? That bandage looks mighty clean to have traveled so fur."

"I fixed it," Jason said. "His arm was broke."

"Don't look broke now," Abner said in surprise.

"I set it."

Abner pushed him aside and took the wounded man's good arm over his own shoulder. "What this army needs," he said drily, "is a few more fourteen-year-old lads . . . like this one." He winked at Eph. "I'll take the feller back to the surgeon. He's got some wagons back a ways, I think."

They came upon two more fugitives before the day was over. One was a Frenchman from the town, who spoke excitedly of the battle. "The general—he is not in the town wiz others; he sit beside the rivière. And so he is quickly catch. These men in the town, they fight well! They say to the British 'Go away, we can hold zis town forever!' But then the General Winchester he send word

"Lean on me and take your weight off'n that leg."

to give up the town!" He flung his hands into the air in a gesture of complete bewilderment.

The men were angered when they heard this. "Just because he got captured hisself was no reason to knuckle down for everybody else!" one man cried indignantly. "Always knew he was a coward!"

"Mebbe not a coward, but a fool, certainly," Eph said. "I heard Major Madison was in command of the town. He could prob'ly have held out if he'd been left alone."

"Yes, yes!" the Frenchman cried. "Already many red-coats are falling—one hundred, two hundred, perhaps—many men. And the Americans in the town, they lose only five-six men!"

Abner shook his head violently, as if to clear it of cob-webs. "It don't make sense," he said gloomily. "If we were winning, why should we surrender?"

Andy said angrily, "Why did Hull surrender last August? Snug in his fort, with plenty of supplies and ammunition, plenty of men—he could ha' held out for months! Yet he handed over Detroit without even firin' a shot!"

Abner said what was in all their minds. "It's the gen-erals that are losin' this war for us! We got some good officers, like this Madison and Colonel Lewis, and such, and one good general—Harrison. Leastways in this part of the country."

"I reckon all wars are full of mistakes, and this one's

no different," Eph said with a sigh. "My pa fought in the Revolution, and he said the same."

The last fugitive they came upon was one who had been found by others, and who was being returned to the base at the Portage River. He was so exhausted he could hardly talk, for he had floundered through deep snow for miles, and fear had taken as great toll of his strength as hardship.

He was a young man, scarcely twenty, but his face wore a hunted, frightened look which aged him considerably. "He's all of atremble," Sergeant Hawkes told them. "Can't git a word of sense out'n him. You'd think he'd never seen a scalpin' before, the way he acts."

"Mebbe he never did," Eph retorted. "I never did myself, nor did Jason here. I can't speak for the others. But no one knows how he'll act in battle till the time comes. This poor lad should never ha' left Kentucky."

The sergeant checked over his men without answering. "We're to fall back to the Portage River," he said at last. "I doubt we'll find any more that have escaped. Seems like only thirty or so got away. Out of a thousand," he added heavily. The men said nothing, but their faces were grim. "The gen'l is holin' up at the Portage till he gits his army in some order."

"And then we'll march on Malden?" Andy asked eagerly.

"No doubt!" the sergeant said with elaborate sarcasm. "We'll all ride there in sleighs and surprise the British.

Surprise ourselves, too!" His gesture toward the deep snow was eloquent. "How you goin' to git an army through that—all the way to Malden? This here blizzard lasted three days, and it ain't goin' to melt off in a hurry."

Andy was silenced.

Back at the Portage River encampment, Jason hunted for Dineen to thank him for his words of recommendation. The ranger was squatting in front of a small lean-to, oiling his rifle with loving fingers. He seemed scarcely to have heard Jason's stammering thanks, and the lad stood there, first on one foot and then on the other, unsure of whether he should stay or depart.

At last Dineen looked up, and his eyes were twinkling. "You're a real woodsman," he said, "so I wasn't doin' *you* a kindness. I was tryin' to help the army!" Then, sobering, "You have a brother Robert?"

"Aye! He's a lot older than me, but—"

"Thought so. He was at Tippecanoe. So was I." He bent to his work again, but a flicker of a smile crossed his lips as he said, "That fust fellow you found in the woods and brought in—he's over there with the other sick ones. Why don't you go see him?"

Jason squirmed. He hadn't looked up the man because he was afraid he might be the object of thanks, and that would embarrass him. But if Dineen thought he should go, he would go.

He turned away and went reluctantly to stand in the

doorway of the building which served as hospital for the wounded. The surgeon's mate looked up from his work over a recumbent form. "Bring me that basin over there!"

Jason brought it. "Now, hold him down while I change the dressing." Jason did his best, but he was not strong enough to hold the writhing man still. He said, without thinking, "I could change the dressing if you could hold him."

Startled, the surgeon's mate opened his mouth to berate Jason, but then he shut it again, and changed places with him. Jason worked quickly, sponging the ugly wound and covering it with a fresh piece of lint. When the patient lay back again with a groan of relief, the surgeon's mate looked up.

"Are you the lad who set a broken arm in the woods?" he asked.

Jason flushed. "Yes, I—Did the man come through all right?"

"He did. I got the bullet out of his thigh with no trouble. It was the break that was the worst, and that was all attended to."

"Where is he?"

"Over there."

The surgeon's mate pointed to a dark corner, and Jason went to stare down at the unshaven face of the man he had saved. "You feelin' better?" he asked awkwardly.

"Aye, thanks to you. . . . Listen, lad, have you any

money you could lend me? I lost everythin' at French-town, and I'd like to buy me a twist of 'baccy to ease my sufferin'."

The surgeon's mate came up to them. "Now, no talk-ing, Brinkley," he said. "You're not yet over your fever, and I want you to stay quiet."

"Brinkley!" Jason echoed. He stared at the wounded man a moment. "Were you at Tippecanoe?"

"Aye."

"Then you're the man who borrowed money from my brother, Robert Potter."

The deep-set eyes shifted. "There's other Brinkleys, no doubt."

The surgeon's mate tugged gently at Jason's arm, and he turned away, grinning. He might have saved the man who owed brother Robert money, but he was quite sure of one thing—Robert would never see his money again, no matter how good a recovery Brinkley made.

At the doorway the surgeon's mate said, "The order-lies mean well, but they do not have your skill. Have you had training?"

Jason said, "I've doctored neighbors and their animals many times, but I only know what I've picked up here and there."

"You should study medicine. You have the gift."

"But I—I have no learnin'. I kin read and write—a little—and figger some, but not much. To be a real doc-tor, I'd have to study for years, mebbe."

"They would pass quickly, for you would be doing what you are fitted for," the man said. Then, with a brisk pat on Jason's shoulder, "Well, I must get back to my patients. Any time you want to help, lad, you will be more than welcome."

CHAPTER 6

THAT was how Jason became the right-hand man of the surgeon's mate. When, some time later, the wounded were sent farther south for care, and Jason went on to the rapids of the Maumee with Harrison's army, he had learned many things. Eph declared he was as good as a doctor, any day! But Jason was not so sure. The more he had learned, the more he had come to realize how very much there was to know.

He said, almost sorrowfully, "Not me, Eph. I reckon Lucy was right, and I'd have to go to school and git me some book learnin' before I could even begin to be a doctor."

Abner spoke up with surprise. "Lucy said that? Wonder what's happened to the little lady. She was right smart, and her pa, too, even though he *was* reg'lar army."

"Well, he wasn't smart enough to leave her home, where she belongs. The major may be moved up to the front any time, and if she goes with him, she might run into real danger." Eph sounded scornful.

"No more'n other lasses have in their day," Abner retorted.

"They were mostly pioneer folk, and used to hardship. Lucy's had a tender upbringin'."

Jason did not join in the conversation, because he agreed with both of them. Lucy, he felt, should never have accompanied her father to this war. At the same time, he had to admit that she had fit into the life at Upper Sandusky without any apparent difficulty. She had pluck, and she was also more practical than he imagined most ladies were.

He wondered about her on the way to the Rapids, and he thought of her several times in the days that followed, as General Harrision set his men to work to build a new fort eighteen miles below the rapids, and across the river from the scene of Anthony Wayne's victory at Fallen Timbers nineteen years before.

The new fort was to be named for the governor of Ohio, Return Jonathan Meigs. Although Abner was disdainful of the efforts of the newly arrived militia from Virginia and Pennsylvania, he admitted he was glad the little army on the Maumee had had its numbers increased to eighteen hundred men.

"Not that they'll be much use," he grumbled, "with such short enlistments. Just when the gen'l will be needin' 'em, they'll trot off home. You wait and see."

"Well, they're here now, and helpin' build Fort Meigs," Eph said, in his mild way. "And if they weren't here the work would be twice as hard for us."

There was plenty of work. Captain Wood, the engineer in charge of the designing and building of the fort, had laid out a plan which called for eight blockhouses with double timbers, four large batteries for the cannon, and an encampment twenty-five hundred yards in circumference, all of it fortified.

Things were only well started when word came that there were six hundred Indians gathered on the north shore of Maumee Bay. This was much too close for comfort, and Harrison took a third of his men, with one cannon, and led them personally. Eph and Abner were crestfallen that they were not among those chosen to go.

But there was no fighting, after all, for as soon as the Americans neared the Indian camp, the savages fled toward Fort Malden on the Canadian side. Although they were pursued, there was no battle.

"I signed up to fight, not cut down trees," Abner grumbled. He was not alone. There were many others who found the hard labor demanded by the building of the fort far from their liking. When their enlistments were up, most men left eagerly for their homes.

"What did I tell you?" Abner said. "In no time at all, we'll be down to five hundred men, and no fort built for shelter agin the Injuns. I've a mind to quit, myself."

But Jason and Eph knew that he was only talking. Abner was not the quitting kind.

Jonathan Dodge went, though. They were not sorry to see the last of him, for he had complained incessantly about everything, and he had managed to avoid any duty that was onerous. The opinion of most was that he would be scared green if it came to a fight.

James Dineen warned him not to go. "I've just come in from a spying trip," he said, "and there's plenty of Injuns about. In small bands—three, four, or half a dozen. You'll more'n likely run into one of 'em." He, too, had scant use for Jonathan, but felt he ought to give the information.

"I'll dodge 'em," Jonathan said cockily, tucking a leather purse full of money into his blouse.

"Well, Dodge is your name, so mebbe you will." The ranger turned away, his duty done.

Jonathan left on a gray morning, and Jason went to help the surgeon's mate, as usual. This was an older man who was not as sympathetic as the one at Portage River, but he was glad of Jason's help, nevertheless.

There were plenty of sick men. The ailments varied—frostbitten feet and hands; bad cuts, where an axe had slipped from numbed fingers; several patients had an inflammation of the lungs. And there was always camp fever.

Jason was about to go to the hospital one afternoon when Eph stopped him. Eph was on fatigue duty that day. He pushed his hair back from his eyes and grinned at his brother. "Bet you can't guess who's come."

"Is the gen'l back?" Jason asked eagerly. All the men felt better when their commander was at the post, but he had left some time ago for Cincinnati. Both Eph and

Abner had been appalled at the laxness which followed his departure, for the men not only stopped most of their work, they had even, in the February cold, used a lot of the pickets for firewood. Much of the work that had already been done on the fort was actually destroyed.

"Not the gen'l," Eph said, "but somebody almost as good. *He*'ll make things hum again."

"Who?"

"Cap'n Wood." Wood was the engineer who had designed the fort. "But that's not who I meant. This'll be a *real* surprise! Major Vernon's here. Come in this afternoon with a detachment."

Jason's face lit up, then sobered again. "I don't s'pose Lucy's with him," he said.

"Sure she is, prettier than ever, and ridin' Diana. She saw me workin' and asked about you fust thing."

"She did! Where is she?"

"They're sharin' a house with a couple other officers—that one over there, behind the house Harrison uses when he's here."

Jason ran. Whatever qualms he might have had concerning Lucy were gone, for she had asked about him "fust thing." That meant she had forgiven him for his rudeness at Upper Sandusky.

She was directing her father's waiter in the disposition of their luggage, and turned quickly as soon as she heard his voice. "Jason!" she cried. "How you've grown!"

"I have?" He looked down at himself in surprise, suddenly realizing that his hunting shirt *was* getting tight across the chest and shoulders.

"You look fine. I think army life agrees with you. Perhaps you should enlist in the regulars," she teased him.

"Not me!" He flushed with pleasure that they were back on the old footing. "Wear one of those heavy old uniforms? And that crazy hat that does nothin' a hat should do? And carry a heavy musket? And run at the trot whenever some officer barks at me? No, ma'am!"

She laughed happily. "You haven't changed very much, after all," she admitted. "What are you doing—hunting?"

He said, somewhat embarrassed, for he knew she would be pleased, "I'm helpin' at the hospital. I helped at the Portage River blockhouse, and now I'm helpin' here—a little. Not as much as I'd like, though."

"Why, Jason," she said, "I think that's wonderful. I've known, ever since you treated Diana's leg, that you have the gift of healing. It must come easy for you, I'm sure."

"No," he told her, "it don't come as easy as I'd thought it would. The simple things, yes. Like cleanin' up a wound, or bandagin', or handin' out the medicine and gittin' it down the men who don't want it. But there's so much I don't know. Why, the surgeon here uses words I never even heard of."

He sighed, and glanced at Lucy, then looked away

quickly again. "I reckon you were right, and I'll have to git book learnin' before I kin hope to be a doctor. But I don't know where I'll ever git it. Eph and I don't live near any schools, and I—"

Lucy said, as if divining what was coming next, "Don't give up the idea, Jason! Please don't! There are plenty of people with education, but not many who have the inborn gift. And you have. I know it!"

He nodded. "So I reckon all I kin do is go on treatin' the neighbors and their critters, the way I used to," he said gloomily.

"If you want an education, you can get it," Lucy said positively. Her voice was almost stern. "And you can start right now. You come here every morning, and we'll have lessons. I've promised to teach one of the officer's children, and you might as well learn something now. Later on, when you've mastered the important beginnings, you can go on from there on your own, until it's time to apprentice yourself to a real doctor."

Jason flushed uncomfortably. "I—I can't pay very much," he said. "I don't git paid by the army, you know. I don't even git rations like the rest of the militia, on account of bein' too young. But Eph and I always manage. I hunt, so that takes care of the food. And I trade some of the game for other things I need. But—but I have hardly any money."

"Did I offer to pay for that lovely fan you made?" she cried, her eyes flashing. "Who mentioned money? I'm *inviting* you to be my pupil!" She added, as she saw the stubborn set of his jaw, "And if you want to bring in any game once in a while, I'm sure it would be welcome."

Lucy proved to be a good teacher. Perhaps because he wanted to shine in her estimation, Jason did better at his

lessons than he had thought he could. Lucy borrowed anything in the way of reading matter that she could from the officers her father knew, and Jason, his brow furrowed, and his tongue feeling twice as thick as usual, would stumble through the collection—accounts in newspapers, poetry, handwritten recipes, anything at all.

There was not much time for hunting, though, unless he cut his time at the hospital. This bothered him, but the surgeon in charge had evidently been told of the lessons by Major Vernon, for he spoke of it one day. "Now that you are starting on the long road to becoming a doctor," he said seriously, "you had best start learning Latin and Greek."

Jason positively paled. "Latin and Greek? What for? I'm havin' enough trouble with my native tongue!"

"What for? Most medical terms come from one or the other language, and unless you have a good grounding in them you would not know what you, or some other doctor, was talking about," the surgeon said with a hint of a smile.

"But why not have 'em in English?" Jason protested. "It don't make sense to have 'em in a foreign language— *two* languages, at that!"

"Oh, yes, it does," the surgeon told him, "for these are the universal terms used throughout the entire civilized world."

"But I don't aim to do any doctorin' except right here in Ohio!"

The surgeon shook his head. "Have you any idea how many different names the simplest herb may have? In Kentucky it will be one thing, in Marietta another, and in Indiana a third. Yet the doctors in all those places call it by the same name—the botanical name. That is why you must know your Latin and Greek."

"Sounds like a lot of work for nothin'," Jason said rebelliously. "I'd sooner learn the different folk-names myself. But if that's the way a doctor has to call it, I'll learn it."

"Well spoken," the surgeon said. "You'll be a doctor yet."

CHAPTER 7

Early one evening, when Jason was about to go to the hospital for a last look about, to see if he could make any of the men more comfortable, Eph stopped him. Jason thought his brother looked excited.

"Wait a minute!" Eph called out.

"What for?"

"The gen'l is sendin' an expedition against the British navy at Malden. The ships are froze fast in the ice, and here's our chance to blow 'em sky high. With their navy gone, we'll be able to capture Malden, and then the invasion of Canada kin git under way."

"Hmp!" Jason was skeptical. "Gen'l Harrison was goin' to do that a couple weeks ago, and couldn't. The ice was too thin."

"Well, they think it's thicker now. We'll likely make it this time."

Jason's heart sank. "You mean—you're goin' with the men that's sent?" he asked.

"You, too. I fixed it. You're to work with Dineen. He asked for you."

74

As quickly as it had sunk, Jason's heart rose again. "When do we leave?" he demanded. "I kin be ready in no time flat."

"Tomorrow mornin', fust thing. That's why I wanted to tell you, so's you'd git some sleep. You'll be needin' it."

The men were to travel in sleighs and cross frozen Lake Erie by way of the Bass Islands. The sleighs were to be left at Middle Bass Island, and the men were to go forward, under cover of darkness, to blow up the British ships.

They were one hundred and forty strong, with explosives prepared by Captain Cushing and six days' provisions. The sleighs bumped over the snowy, half-mired roads. All of the roads were strewn with stumps and fallen logs. It was much better on the ice of the lake but James Dineen, with whom Jason was riding, shook his head.

"Don't like the looks of that ice," he said once. "It's got a watery look to it."

Jason stared at the ice, but it looked the same as any ice to him. He was not acquainted with any lake as large as Lake Erie, and the ice he had seen on creeks and small rivers was different, somehow.

"It's been a queer winter," he said now. "Seems as if the weather was set against our gittin' to Canada, don't it?"

"No use blamin' the weather for anythin'," Dineen

said. "Men were at fault most times." He paused so long that Jason thought he had forgotten the subject, and then Dineen said in a rush, "Men that wouldn't stay a minute beyond their service time, so that when a good-sized army was needed there wasn't but a few companies left. And men that cheated on food and blankets and clothin' for the soldiers, so they was discontented and all too ready to leave fust chance they had. And men in high places that didn't know—or forgot, which was wuss —what the enemy was like, and so they put themselves and their armies in bad positions, or surrendered 'em to be butchered by the Injuns. . . . It's mostly men to blame, lad, not the weather."

But it *was* the weather this time, as they discovered, for the lake, instead of being completely frozen over, had too much open water for them to cross to Malden, and they were forced to return.

"Seems like we'll never git to Canada," Abner remarked gloomily when they were back in Fort Meigs.

"We've already done it—under Hull," Eph reminded him.

"Oh, that!" Utter disgust was in Abner's voice. "And what did the army do? What were they allowed to do? Sat still for four weeks in Canada, so's to give the British time to destroy bridges and put up defenses. And even when Colonel Cass marched ahead towards Malden, and had a chance to make the Canadians knuckle under, what did Hull do? Left him there, without support or reinforcements, and then told him to come back so's all the Americans could retreat to Detroit. I tell you, when I heard that I near turned agin my own gov'ment for sendin' such a numbskull to command our men!"

"I reckon everybody with sense felt the same way," Eph said with a sigh. "Now the British are dug in

for fair, with plenty of Injuns to help 'em—thanks to Tecumseh—and we're goin' to have a hard time to git anywhere in this war. Like as not the British'll invade us fust."

"They're goin' to have a hard time findin' us," Jason said with a chuckle. "Less they stir around in the mud!"

The others grinned wryly. For days there had been rain that, combined with the melting of the snow and ice, had turned the fort into a sea of mud, more than eight inches deep in most places. Men who started to head for home when their enlistments expired, had to return a few days later, with stories of a sea of water over the countryside not a mile from the fort. The river was swollen beyond recognition, and cattle and hogs and horses were engulfed by the waters and lost.

The wet brought on a host of ailments, and for the next few weeks Jason was busy helping the doctor, for the number of patients increased daily. Men had chest coughs, and severe rheumatism, and fevers induced by the moisture and by chilling.

He was faithful in going for his lessons every day, and Lucy told him he was making good progress. But he still felt his lack of basic knowledge keenly, and went about his work reciting the next day's exercise from Webster's Elementary Spelling Book. Jason worked on his sums in the evenings, using a piece of charcoal and a smooth piece of wood. Sometimes, when he thought of all there was to be learned before he could even begin to apprentice himself to a doctor, he became so discouraged that he was tempted to give up the whole idea.

But he knew he could not face Lucy with this decision. Nor could he face her with his lessons unlearned, so he studied harder than he would have thought possible, and applied himself to them whenever he had a free moment.

Lucy felt penned up in the fort, he knew. It was bad enough that it was too dangerous for her to venture outside the pickets. What was worse was that she could scarcely get about inside the fort because of the mud and the frantic work of fortification that was going on. She performed little household tasks, but most of the chores were taken off her shoulders by her father's waiter and by the woman who shared their lodging.

Jason found that Lucy was particularly eager to hear him tell of his experiences in the woods. "Adventures," she called them, although he had never thought of them in that light, since they were part of his daily life. She asked so many questions one day that he said, on impulse, "Now that you've been kind enough to teach me, Miss Lucy, mebbe I kin repay you a little when we've finer weather by teachin' you a few of the tricks of the woods."

"I'd like that!" she said instantly. "Oh, I wish the sun would come out for good and dry up all this mud! What will you teach me, Jason?"

He thought for a minute. "Well, fust off, you should learn how to walk so's you're not heard and you're not seen. That's important in this country, when a body never knows what's behind the next bush."

"You mean, stalk like an Indian?"

"An Injun stalks for prey. I doubt you'll be doin' that," he said with a grin. "No, you'd best learn how to move so's an Injun can't stalk *you*."

"Well, what should I do? Show me now," she begged.

Jason felt embarrassed. He looked at the puncheon floor with a quizzical eye. It was hardly the same as a forest floor, he thought wryly, but maybe if he gave her the general idea, she'd be better able to practice when the weather was kinder.

He looked down at her, and realized how much he had grown in these few months, for she seemed smaller than ever. Her fine woolen dress, with its trimming of velvet ribbon, seemed incongruous in this wilderness fortress. Yet he knew that Lucy had grit. Her inner strength was concealed by a feminine manner and only showed in the way she took the rough life, without complaining and with a natural dignity.

How to teach her? And did she really want to learn, or was she only asking him to do this so that he would not feel too deeply in debt to her? Jason sighed. He scarcely knew where to begin, for the things he wanted to tell her were things he had known as long as he could remember.

She was waiting patiently, her eyes wide with questions. He said, abruptly, "Fust off, you must never move fast unless you're runnin' from danger. And then you'd better put the wind in your heels."

She dimpled. "Well, that much I knew."

"But about the movin' slow—that's important. The minute you move too fast, the game knows you're there. Lots of animals see best by noticin' movement."

"Yes," she nodded, "that makes sense."

"Never stop lookin', and listenin', and smellin'. That's the next thing."

"Smelling!" she echoed. "Smelling what?"

He threw his arms wide to emphasize what he said. "Everythin'!"

She wrinkled her brow a little. "All right, I'll go about smelling. But what good will that do, when I won't even know what it is that I'm smelling?"

"There you are!" he said triumphantly. "That's the sort of thing I can't teach you till we kin git outside. But the weather'll change sometime. It's got to."

She dismissed the weather with a shake of her curls. "What's next?"

"Let's see. . . . The way you walk. That's somethin' you have to practice a lot, though. If you put your foot down wrong, you make a noise. Break a twig on the ground, or rustle dry leaves. That kin give you away before you know what you've done. You have to put your weight down easy—like this." He demonstrated,

82 THE PROVING YEARS

walking across the small room with a flowing, catlike tread.

Lucy cocked her head, watching him, then followed after him. "No, no," he said quickly, "you're too stiff in the knees. That's too much of a lady's walk. It's pretty as all get out, but a body could hear you comin' in the woods before he saw you!"

Lucy took his criticism with good grace, and tried again. Before he left her house that morning, Jason had the satisfaction of having watched her cross the room with silent, smooth movements.

The exchange of lessons went on from that day. While Jason battled with the rule of three, Lucy practiced walking toe first, then heel first, and crouching low behind the trestle table.

"Never look over the top of a bush or rock," Jason said sternly when she rose cautiously to peer over the edge. "Look out low and sideways."

"Like this?" she asked him, crawling on hands and knees to the side and slowly poking her head around the corner.

"That's it. Only you should ha' looked from the other side of the table," he warned her. "The light from the window throws your shadder out ahead of you on this side. Always remember your shadder!"

A voice behind him made him jump. "And why should she remember her shadow?" It was Lucy's father, Major Vernon.

Lucy clapped her hands with joy. "Oh, Jason!" she crowed. "*You* weren't looking, and listening, and smelling that time, or you would have known Father was there."

Jason scrambled to his feet, his face red. "Wind was the wrong way," was all he could say, and the major joined his daughter in laughter.

Major Vernon had not known that Lucy was taking lessons in woodcraft, and now that the secret was out, Lucy insisted on showing him what she had learned. He watched her with a serious face, nodding when she explained each step of her training to him.

"I don't know too much of woodland lore myself," he admitted when she had finished. "And in this part of the country, I feel it is a good thing to know. If I weren't so busy, Jason, I might take some lessons from you myself."

CHAPTER 8

By the middle of March there were several deaths in the fort every day. Men lay in mud and water in their tents. There was no wood for fuel; the timber had been cut off for some distance around the fort. The teams had no forage, and so they were too weak to haul wood from the forest.

Every few days a man was reported missing. A lieutenant was found shot and scalped, his body thrust under the river ice. A scouting party crossed the river to hunt for Indian signs, and one of the men failed to return. There was little doubt in the minds of the men at Fort Meigs that they were being watched constantly by the Indians who were allies of the British.

But at least the fish had begun to bite. This meant a welcome addition to their diet, and many of the men risked Indian attacks to do a little fishing in the Maumee.

April brought no relief from the Indian menace. Although reinforcements came, it was not until General Harrison arrived from the southern part of the state that men's spirits revived. In jubilation at their commander's approach, the artillery fired fifteen guns as a salute.

Things began to move faster with Harrison on the

scene. Officers as well as soldiers were employed in building breastworks, repairing pickets, digging a well, removing stumps, and laying blockhouse floors. The place throbbed with activity.

Jason helped, like everyone else, and his lessons had to be foregone for a while. But he still managed to appear at the hospital every day, to do the chores he knew were necessary, and for which there never seemed to be enough men. And he still recited his lessons under his breath, for the more he saw of sickness and death, the more he was determined to become a doctor someday.

On the sixteenth, a party of spies was sent out to go down-river, keeping a lookout for British and Indians, and another party was sent to the River Raisin on the same errand. Dineen was in this second group, as were Eph and Jason. They moved swiftly through the woods and swamp, yet with the inborn caution of well-trained woodsmen, and met three Frenchmen who said that Tecumseh, the great Shawnee leader, had passed that way only the day before. He had eighty Indians with him, and was on his way to the British stronghold at Malden.

The Frenchmen said that it was understood the British and Indians would attack Fort Meigs within ten or twelve days. With this news, the party hastened to return to the fort, bringing the Frenchmen with them.

They were crossing a creek, still roaring from the spring thaws, when Dineen slipped on a wet rock. Jason was behind him and saw him strike his head on a stone as he fell. The force of the rushing water rolled Dineen over and over, and bore him downstream at a frightening rate of speed.

Jason thrust his rifle into the hands of his brother behind him, and plunged into the water. Slipping, sliding, falling, half-swimming, he went after the unconscious ranger, while Eph ran along the bank, hoping to intercept Dineen before Jason could reach him.

But it was Jason who got to him first. He caught hold of Dineen's belt and dragged him toward the steep bank. Eph scrambled down to help him, several other rangers following.

Dineen was battered and bruised but, once he was brought to his senses, he swore that he was fit enough to go on with the best of them. Jason bore almost as many bruises as the man he had saved, but he did not complain, either, and insisted on carrying his rifle once more. He marched alongside Dineen for a while, to make sure that the older man was able to keep up with the group.

They had gone more than a mile before Dineen spoke. Then he said only, "Guess I had real foresight, askin' you to come along. Always knew you was a good man in the woods." That was his thanks, but Jason understood and was proud. They were all seasoned men in this little expedition, yet it was he, the youngest and least experienced of all, who had saved Dineen's life.

The news they brought back to the fort, and which the Frenchmen retailed again to General Harrison, only confirmed the general's expectations. Work went ahead every day and all day on the great traverses across the enclosed ground of the fort. Breastworks were thrown up against the pickets, making them almost impregnable. There were cross-traverses, too, so that the men could go in safety from one part of the fort to another without exposing themselves to enemy fire. The ammunition was all placed in safe magazines underground. With the arrival of every pack train bearing provisions, and with the additional troops which still poured in, the men at Fort Meigs felt more confident.

On the twenty-sixth, the first British and Indians made their appearance across the river. Jason was called out of the hospital the next morning by Sergeant Hawkes.

"Think you could go out and bring back some word of what's goin' on down there?" The sergeant pointed across the river and downstream. "Stick to this side of the river and count the troops, if you see any. And bring your scalp back where it belongs, lad."

He seemed to have no doubt of Jason's willingness to take the assignment, since he did not even wait to find out if the boy wanted to go. With a pat on the back, and repeating the watchword and countersign, he sent Jason off on his dangerous errand.

Jason, well aware of the fact that he might be observed from the moment of his departure, took elaborate precautions. He scarcely moved for minutes at a time, and then went sideways as often as he went forward. When he had won the cover of the trees, he was bolder, but now every sense was sharpened. Now, indeed, he was practicing what he had told Lucy—looking, listening, smelling. The wind was in his favor, but that meant that, if it did not veer, it would be against him on his return.

Once he felt himself safe from observation, Jason went faster. Approaching the river several miles below the fort, he suddenly threw himself flat upon the ground. There, anchored in the river, were a number of vessels flying the British flag. There were two gunboats, and a brig, as well as many smaller ships.

Then the British really were going to besiege Fort Meigs! Jason tried to estimate the number of men on each ship, but knew that he was only guessing. He hoped the sergeant would have some idea if he could tell him about the boats and give him accurate descriptions of their size and number. He lay in the grass, memorizing the scene before him, and then turned back.

Perhaps it was because he was in such a hurry to return to the fort and report what he had seen. Perhaps it was because the ground was broken and hard to cross at that point, and he was distracted from his usual caution. Whatever it was, Jason was only a mile or so from the fort when there was a shot behind him.

The ball whistled harmlessly over his head, but only because he had stooped at that moment to avoid an overhanging branch. With the movement of a startled animal, he leaped to one side and sought shelter behind a tree. Crouching behind adjacent bushes, and then crawling on his belly to take cover behind a boulder, Jason felt as if his ears must be sticking out two feet from his head. Every sound that he heard held a separate meaning.

The chatter of a squirrel, high in the tree behind which he had first dodged; the snapping of a twig as a rabbit, frightened by his approach, bounded away; the whisper of the first green leaves in a sudden little gust of wind. But there was no other sound.

Jason was quite sure that the man who had fired at him must be near, but he had no idea where. One thing was sure—that man had not stayed where he was any more than Jason had stayed where he had been. And was there only one man? Or were there several, and were they around him, waiting for some faint sign so that they could close in?

He decided that his best chance for survival lay in being absolutely quiet, not moving so much as a hair, and breathing as quietly as he could. This might be a waiting game, and if it was, he was pretty sure he could outlast the other man.

The minutes dragged on and still there was no sound, either from his hiding place or from any other spot.

Since the wind was against him, Jason was unable to tell by his nose whether it was a white man or an Indian who was stalking him. He thought he might have to stay in this one spot all night, but he was prepared to do it, rather than give himself away.

In the end, his patience paid. The other man, becoming increasingly curious, made the first movement. It was so faint, and so distant that if Jason had not had every sense alerted, he would have missed it. But a leaf stirred where no other leaves stirred. And then the coloring behind the leaf shifted slightly. Where it had been brown, it became red, and then, briefly, black and white, and then brown again.

There was an Indian behind that bush, that was sure. An Indian who had painted his face red. Jason moved his rifle forward, an eighth of an inch at a time, his eyes never leaving the spot where he had seen the movement. When minutes had passed, and he had his rifle stock couched beneath his chin, he decided to risk a shot.

But when he pressed the trigger, there was only a click. The rifle had misfired! This meant trouble, and he knew it, for the enemy facing him had surely heard that click and had placed him from the sound. He waited for the answering shot, knowing that it would come, and pressed himself even flatter against the earth. He wished that he could melt into it, but was thankful that he lay in a slight depression, which was almost as good.

This was to be a duel to the death.

When the shot did come, it sailed above him. The rock was a real protection. But at once there was a loud whoop as the Indian warrior leaped from his hiding place and came forward on the run, tomahawk in hand.

Jason jumped to his feet and ran. He zigzagged from side to side, taking whatever cover offered itself, and once he found another rock, he dodged behind it. It was not a moment too soon, for the tomahawk whizzed through the air and clanged upon the rock. It spun into the air and Jason, making a leap after it, caught it as it came down again.

Now he turned to face the Indian. The warrior stood boldly, disdaining to hide, and still sounding his war cry. Jason saw, to his dismay, that the man had a second tomahawk, and in his other hand he clutched a knife. Jason threw the tomahawk he was holding with all his force. The Indian swerved slightly, so that it missed him.

Now Jason had only his knife left. He felt a surge of excitement. This was to be a duel to the death, but he was unafraid. Keeping his eyes fixed on the Indian, he stooped and picked up a small rock he felt under his foot. The Indian, thinking him off balance, threw his second tomahawk, but Jason was prepared, and leaped to one side. At the same moment, he threw his rock.

It caught the Indian unawares, and struck him full in the face. He dropped without a sound.

Jason watched him for a full minute before he came

out from behind the sheltering rock. The Indian did not stir. Jason's ears were alert for any sound. Had the whooping brought other Indians to the scene? If so, from which direction would they be coming?

As he approached the Indian slowly, circling so that he would come upon him from behind, he noticed what had puzzled him before. The black and white he had glimpsed so briefly behind the moving leaf, was a fine belt of wampum—more black than white, which made it more valuable—that the Indian wore.

Jason stared down at the red-painted warrior. The man still breathed, but faintly. He knew that many of the Ohio men would not have hesitated to take the Indian's scalp, but that was something he disapproved of. White men who did such things were no better than the Indians they hated and reviled.

No, what he wanted from this Indian was that belt of wampum. He let himself grin a little, the tension and excitement of the past half hour fading now. It would be something to hand Lucy Vernon for all her trouble in giving him lessons.

When he came back to the fort, the sentinel eyed the strip of purple-and-white shell beads with a knowing cock of the head. "You been out tradin' with the Injuns?" he asked with a laugh.

Jason laughed in return. "You might call it that," he said. But he did not explain.

Sergeant Hawkes was waiting for him. "You been

gone a long time—" he began, then broke off as he spied the wampum. "Where'd you git that?" he demanded, his bushy eyebrows shooting up in surprise.

"Off an Injun," Jason said with assumed casualness.

The sergeant gave him a keen glance. "You don't git that kind of wampum off a live Injun, without givin' him plenty in return," he said.

Jason smiled. "Did I say he was a live Injun?" he asked innocently.

CHAPTER 9

The siege opened before dawn on May first. The artillery on the British gunboats began firing then, but the ships lay too far down-river for the shots to do any damage.

For several days the British, under Proctor, had been engaged in establishing their batteries across the river. Now, when the sun was well up, these began firing, too. The Americans had been using their artillery for some time in an effort to discourage the placing of these batteries, and in throwing grape and cannister shot at the Indians who were at the rear of the fort and deployed along the flanks.

On that first day the British sent over two hundred and forty shot and shells, but did very little damage. Now the general's wisdom in ordering the digging of the traverses was revealed, for men could cross the campground with comparative safety, and the little rooms that had been dug out along the traverses served as safe places to rest and sleep.

The American guns spoke in return with heavy fire. The din was tremendous. Cannoneers swaggered when they were off duty (which was seldom), feeling themselves the real saviors of the place. The infantry laughed back. "Wait till they storm the fort!" one of them yelled in derision. "A lot of good your big guns'll be then! You'll be beggin' us to save your skins with our rifles and muskets!"

Jason was busier than usual. With the influx of wounded, the surgeon in charge of the hospital was glad to have the help of two extra hands. Especially since they were willing hands, and dexterous, as well. Jason watched while the surgeon probed for splinters or bullets, and tried not to hear the shrieks when a limb was amputated.

He turned away from one of the wounded on the second day of the siege, and almost bumped into Lucy. She wore a heavy coverall over her fine woollen dress, and her curls were slightly disheveled.

"Lucy!" he cried. "What are you doin' here? Is your pa hurt?"

"No, thank heaven," she answered. "But I couldn't remain at home with so much work to be done here, could I?"

Jason thought there were many officers' daughters who might well have stayed away from such unpleasant scenes, and sounds, and smells, feeling themselves too delicate to be exposed to pain and horror. But he thought, too, that this offer of help was no more than he would have expected from Lucy.

She said, as if to take his attention from her, "Sergeant Hawkes was looking for you. I am surprised that he did not come here—he knows that you are always helping at the hospital."

Jason wondered what the formidable sergeant could be wanting of him, but as he was busy, and the sergeant did not come for him, he decided it was a matter of small moment. That night, when he huddled in the small dugout which he shared with his brother and Andy and Abner, he referred to the message Lucy had given him.

"He wanted someone young and spry enough to dodge between the cannon balls, I reckon," Abner said. "If we keep on bombardin' the British, we'll be runnin' out of cannon balls for the twelve and eighteen-pounders. They're offerin' a gill of whiskey for every ball found in those sizes and returned to the magazine."

Eph said, "I thought, when I heard about it, we might have more men outside the walls than in, but it hasn't been so. Too hot for 'em to go wanderin' around lookin' for cannon balls. The Injuns on the right flank have been shootin' like mad all day." He shrugged. "So long as they don't hit too many of us, I'm just as glad they're wastin' their ammunition."

They found out, the next day, why the Indians had kept up such a heavy fire. A new British battery opened up on the fort. It was not more than three hundred yards away, and on the Fort Meigs side of the river.

"Small wonder they were firin' like that," Andy said,

with a nod of his head. "It was to cover up for their artillery placement. If we'd had sense, we would ha' made a sortie out that way to find out what they were about."

"Hindsight is always wise," Abner said with a grin. "Accordin' to you, we didn't have sense. And I'm afeared you're right. So now we got shot and bombs comin' at us from this side, too." He looked sideways at Eph. "Want to earn a couple gills of whiskey, Eph? I'm willin' to try if you are."

"I'll go, too," Jason said at once. He did not like the idea of his brother facing such danger alone.

"You stay here," Eph said with real sternness, and Jason, who had seldom heard that note in his voice, was taken aback.

"If you kin go, so kin I," he said sturdily, and his brother made a sudden gesture of resignation.

Jason was startled. He had not really expected his defiance to get results. It made him realize, as nothing else had, that Eph now considered him a man.

It was exciting, and more than a little frightening, to dash out when a ball had fallen short, and to retrieve it—if it was a cold one—and carry it back into the fort. Sometimes he brought in a ball of the wrong size, but he soon learned, both from the sound and the appearance of the cannon balls, which were the ones wanted by Captain Cushing and his men. When the whiskey was measured out, it was Jason who had earned the most.

"That's 'cause you're younger and sprier than we are," Abner said with a twinkle. "Told you so yestiddy. What you goin' to do with yours?"

"Trade it," Jason answered promptly. And trade it he did, to good advantage, ending up with a fine canteen, an almost new blanket, and a knife that was far better than the one he had had.

Andy snorted when he saw the loot. "You may ha' been dodgin' rifle bullets and spent cannon balls out there," he said, "but we men inside here been dodgin', too. And they haven't paid us extry for it, neither!"

The bombardment was particularly heavy that day and the next, but at break of day on the fifth, they had good news. General Clay was coming with his brigade— more than a thousand men—to reinforce the garrison of the fort.

"They're comin' down the river in boats," Andy cried, almost dancing with excitement. "And most of 'em is goin' to land on the other side of the river, and sneak down onto Proctor's batteries, and spike their guns. *That*'ll finish the British, all right!"

Everyone who could stop work to watch did so, as some of General Clay's men, under Colonel Dudley, surprised the British completely. "They've done it! They've done it!" Jason cried in triumph when the American troops stormed and captured the battery, and he cheered with the others in the fort when the British flag was hauled down. They waited in suspense while

Dudley's Kentuckians, tasting victory, sped after the retreating foe into the forest.

Now Jason was uneasy. Why didn't they come back? He knew that Harrison had ordered them to spike the guns and then come back across the river to the fort at once. But there were only a few stragglers coming to the boats. The others had disappeared into the woods. He thought of the hundreds of Indians concealed in the cover of those woods, and his frown deepened. Kentucky men should not have been so rash. They should have had the memory of Indian raids to make them cautious.

"Here comes Gen'l Clay!" someone yelled, and his attention shifted to the river again. There was shouting

from officers and men and the braying of bugles, as soldiers within the fort were lined up. "We're goin' to git the British batteries on our side of the river!" Andy cried, on the way to his place in the line.

"We got to wait till Clay gits here with his men. And Colonel Boswell's grounded on Turkey Point. He's got the rest of the troops!" Abner yelled, racing along the traverse toward his rendezvous. There was still firing from the batteries on the south side of the river, but with the silencing of the main British batteries, the men scarcely noticed it.

That was an exciting day. The men under Colonel Miller sallied forth to charge upon the enemy, eight hundred and fifty strong. They drove them from their

batteries at bayonet point, spiked their guns, and scattered their forces. They came back, wildly jubilant, with
forty-three prisoners.

It was a sad day, too, for Colonel Dudley and his
men—six hundred of them—had not come back from
the other side of the river. How many of them had
fallen? How many had been captured?

Jason sensed that Miller's sortie would mark the end
of the siege. As he walked slowly toward the hospital,
his thoughts were, strangely, not triumphant at all. He
was thinking of those hundreds captured by the Indians
in Dudley's attack. He was thinking of the many dead.
He was thinking that it did not take long to kill a man.

His work would be with the wounded; he would try,
in his small way, to make them well again. But it would
take so long, and some of them would die, no matter
how much was done for them. Yet what satisfaction
there was to be earned with the healing of one of them.
The conviction grew steadily within him: How much
better it was to cure than to kill!

CHAPTER 10

With full summer upon them, the garrison of Fort Meigs relaxed. There were fish to be caught in the Maumee River, and deer to be hunted in the forest beyond the pickets. Some of the officers had planted gardens with lettuce, and radishes, and peas and beans.

The spring rains were over, and the epidemics of measles and mumps which had struck the troops had died down. In June, when the wild strawberries were red upon the hills, Jason took a kerchief full of them to Lucy.

"Oh, how lovely!" she exclaimed, cupping them in her hands. "I've been so longing for fruit. And you can't imagine how much I want to get out of the fort for a while."

"Won't your pa let you go at all?"

"He says it's too dangerous."

"Well," Jason said slowly, "there's always danger—from something—anywhere. Only there's apt to be a mite more—from the Injuns—here."

She laughed. "That's what he says."

Jason added, "But mebbe if my brother and his friend Abner, and my friend Andy and me, all went with you to protect you, mebbe then he'd let you go."

"I'll ask him!" Lucy cried.

The major was doubtful at first, but on inquiring about the men Jason had mentioned, and on hearing that they were among the best of the militia at the fort, he agreed that she might go. But they must promise to go only a short distance, and to stay only a little while.

It was the first of many excursions. The men's vigilance did not relax, even though the countryside seemed quite peaceful. And now, at last, Jason could give Lucy her lessons in woodcraft in the right surroundings. He was surprised to see how quickly she caught onto everything he told her. She was eager to learn, and he could see that to her this was like a game. Well, he thought, she was entitled to some amusement. She had been cooped up in the fort for a long time, with little to occupy her time but volunteer work at the hospital.

One day he undertook to show her various things which one could eat, even though stranded in the woods without a weapon. Hog peanuts from the damp woodlands, and the fleshy rootstock of the great bulrush in quiet waters. On higher ground there were berries, and an occasional puffball or coral mushroom.

"But how would I make a fire to cook these things?" Lucy asked.

"What I've shown you kin be eaten raw," Jason said, "for if you had no weapon, you'd likely have no means to make a fire, neither."

Lucy made a face. "Ugh! Raw roots and mushrooms!" She shuddered. "I think I'd rather go hungry."

Jason laughed. "That's because you never *have* gone hungry!" he told her.

Several times she begged to be taken to Fort Miamis, the old deserted fort of the British a few miles downriver, but the men refused to go. They had been there themselves several times, to gather cannon balls for their own artillery, and they knew how desolate the place was. There was the mound of a mass burial where many of Dudley's men, captured after their wild onslaught on the north shore batteries, had been slaughtered by the Indians after their surrender. Every time that Jason or his brother and friends went there, they came upon another dead man or two, still unburied, and took that sad duty upon themselves.

It was no place for Lucy, that was sure. Besides, it was too dangerous now, for as the days went by rumors reached them that there would be another attack on the fort. Proctor now had two thousand Canadians and regulars, and anywhere from two to four thousand Indians.

When this news reached Jason and Eph, Eph only said, "That's a lot of Injuns." And Jason added, "I don't think we'd better take Lucy outside the pickets any more."

But there was no need to break this news to Lucy. When Jason went for his daily lesson, she greeted him with a smile that seemed forced. "This will be our last class," she said, almost at once. "Father has been transferred to Fort Defiance. I think perhaps I'm something of a drag on him, Jason," she said quickly, when he would have spoken. "I shouldn't have insisted on coming with him. Then he would not have been sent back to one of the safer forts like this. I'm sure he's quite disappointed, although he tries not to show it."

Jason swallowed hard. Somehow, he had not dreamed of this—that Lucy would be leaving. He said only, "When you goin'?"

"Tomorrow. I'm all packed, though there isn't much to take. But I've put the blue-jay fan where it won't get crushed, Jason, and I shall wear the belt of wampum."

She was trying to soften the blow for him, he knew. He said hoarsely, "Who'll teach me when you're gone?"

"I don't know." Her voice was sad, and there was no longer the pretense of a smile. "But please go on studying, Jason. I'm leaving some books for you because I know that you can learn a great deal by yourself, if you want to. And you must want to."

"I do," he said soberly. "But it's harder that way. . . . You goin' to keep on with your woodland lessons?" But before she could answer, he added, "Best do it indoors. Fort Defiance ain't too far out of the way for the Injuns these days."

Eph noticed his worried look and his unusual silence

that evening as the four men gathered for their supper. "I guess you heard Major Vernon's goin' tomorrow," he said.

Abner looked up, startled. "Miss Lucy, too?" he asked, and when Eph nodded, he said, "That's a smart distance for the little lady to travel. I hope her pa has some good men with him for escort."

No one else said anything, but Jason knew they were all depressed by the news. He was up before dawn the next morning, to curry Diana and to look her over from mane to tail to make sure she was in good condition. Lucy found him in the stables, and he glanced up from his stooped position.

"Don't want her goin' lame on you," he said, to explain his presence.

"She won't. She's in fine shape, only perhaps a little frisky for lack of real exercise," Lucy said. She was her old self today. Maybe she didn't mind going, after all, Jason thought. Maybe she was glad of the change.

Their leave-taking was simple. When her bundle was tied onto the saddle, Jason gave her a hand up. She settled herself comfortably, and smiled down at him. "I'll be back, Jason," she said.

He wondered afterward what she had meant by that. Did she have some news that made her think her pa would be sent back to Fort Meigs? Or was she just trying to be kind, to make him believe they'd meet again? He knew he would miss her very much, and he doubted if he would have the perseverance to stick at his lessons without her prodding.

That afternoon he decided to go hunting upriver. He amused himself by picking out Diana's hoofprints where, occasionally, the party had crossed a muddy section of road. It took expert tracking, and he finally roused himself by saying crossly, "This ain't shootin' anythin' for supper!"

He started into the woods, but the sound of pounding hoofbeats stopped him. Another express from the south, he thought. Sounds urgent. And then, instantly, he leaped back into the roadway, holding up his hand as he recognized the rider. The horse shied around him, almost unseating the rider, who only yelled "Injuns!" before he sped on.

Jason felt his scalp prickle with fear. That man had been one of Major Vernon's escort. The Indian attack must have been on the major's troops. And Lucy was with them! He began to run.

He met the main body of the escort several miles farther on. They were in good order, considering that two of their comrades were dead, and the major was being held upright in the saddle by one of his men. But there was no sign of Lucy.

"Where is she?" Jason shouted as soon as he saw them.

"The Injuns got her!" "Her horse got scairt and ran into the woods, with her on it!" "We hunted for her, but we couldn't find no trace!" Several of them answered him at once. The major did not speak, and Jason saw that his scalp had been creased by a bullet. He seemed to be only half-conscious, and unaware of what was going on about him.

Jason cried, "Give me one of your horses! I'll go after her!"

They didn't want to give up one of their mounts, but he jerked at the reins of one of them and looked so fierce that the trooper dismounted. The men gaped at him. "Where'd it happen?" Jason demanded. "Which way did she go?"

"Back about a mile. You'll see where it is. We got a couple of the varmints."

"She went off to the right," someone else said.

That was toward the river. Did the Indians have canoes? Or did they have horses? He did not wait to find out, but kicked the horse into a gallop.

The place where the attack had taken place was, indeed, easy to find. Jason scarcely noticed the fallen Indians; his eyes were fixed on the ground. He saw the broken twigs where Lucy's horse had dashed into the woods. He followed. For a while the path was easy to see, then, suddenly, there were the tracks of several horses. His heart fell. Had their riders been in pursuit of Lucy, or had they already caught her?

When nightfall came, he tethered his horse, for he did not want to waste time in the morning looking for him. He scarcely slept, waiting with a dreadful impatience for daylight, so that he could go on.

But, although he was up before dawn, his eyes peering through the gloom of the forest, he soon lost the trail in a swamp. He wished that Lucy had had something which she could have dropped along the way, but he knew she had nothing. The Indians had doubtless robbed her of her bundle and were watching her closely. He wondered if they were heading for the River Raisin and then for Detroit, and if they would try to get ransom for her there.

He met the search party on his way back to the fort. Dineen was in the lead, and Eph—a very worried Eph—was beside him. Eph let out a shout when he saw his brother. "Did you find any trace of her?"

"Found it and lost it," Jason said miserably. "They took her into a big swamp, and I lost the trail."

Dineen listened carefully to his story. "We'll spread out in the swamp. Mebbe we kin find somethin'."

But the swamp was too big, and they had to turn back. Jason was silent on the way to the fort, and Eph said little.

It was Dineen who almost stumbled over the body. He let out a grunt, and the rest of the little troop stopped short. "Who is it?" Jason lurched forward, his heart in his mouth for fear it might be Lucy.

"Don't know, but he's been here a long time. Since winter or early spring, I'd say." Dineen stooped over the

Suddenly there were the tracks of several horses.

remains. "Lost his hair, so it was an Injun got him. Hardly any clothes left, either. That makes it an Injun, sure. . . . There's a little leather bag. But it's empty."

Jason peered at it and knew it at once. "It wasn't empty when he left the fort," he said slowly. "But he wouldn't wait to go with the others."

"Who wouldn't?" Dineen asked curiously.

"Jonathan Dodge," Jason said.

Somehow, the sight of that grim skeleton made Jason wonder if Lucy had had any chance at all. Perhaps the Indians had killed her, and he had only been following her horse, while she lay in some deserted spot. Eph glanced at him, and seemed to read his thoughts.

He said, "You know, Jason, those lessons you gave Lucy will come in handy now."

But Jason was not to be comforted.

CHAPTER 11

Pⁱᴏɴᴇᴇʀ folk were used to death and loss, but Jason, as the youngest of his family, had known little of them. Lucy was much more like a sister than either Nan or Tabitha had ever been. Through knowing her he had come to realize how much he and Eph had missed by living as they did—half-camping, half-farming, with little of the gentler side of life to tempt them to change.

He kept his feelings to himself as best he could, but his brother and his friends knew that the thought of Lucy never really left him. If there were not a war on, he would surely have gone after her long since, searching, asking, traveling in the hope of finding her again.

Lucy's father recovered quickly. The bullet had given him a concussion, but he was himself again within a few days. Himself, and yet not himself, for his face showed the ravages of continual worry. He, too, said little, but when he left for Fort Defiance, he bent down from his horse to have a few words with Jason.

"Keep looking for her," he said earnestly. "I feel in my heart that she is still living. And if you should hear anything—the merest rumor—let me know of it."

"I will, sir," Jason promised.

The spirits of the garrison were raised toward the middle of July by word from Commodore Perry who had been building a fleet of American ships at Erie on the lake. The ships were ready now, and furnished with guns and provisions. All that the commodore lacked was men.

"Wish I knew one end of a boat from the other," Abner said when he heard of it. "I'd walk out'n here tomorrow and volunteer."

"It's not likely he'll find any sailors in this neck o' the woods." Eph smiled. "So mebbe you'd be welcome, at that."

They heard that the British navy on Lake Erie, which was based at Malden, was hovering just outside the harbor where Perry's ships lay out of reach of the gunboats, blockading the new little fleet.

"The gen'l says we can't make any real move against Canada till we git rid of the British ships," Andy said. "His waiter told me. So mebbe we *all* ought to walk out'n here and volunteer to be sailors. We'd see some action that way, anyhow!"

But they soon had troubles of their own to worry about. Word came trickling into the fort that Proctor had been persuaded to attack Fort Meigs a second time by the Indian leader, Tecumseh.

"I sort o' wish Gen'l Harrison was here," Abner said, when rumor became fact and the enemy appeared, five thousand strong, at the mouth of the Maumee River. "Gen'l Clay's a fine man, but we had Harrison with us last time, and I felt safer."

"Well, that's a new idea," Eph said with a grin. "I didn't know you went to war to feel safe!"

"You know what I mean!" Abner lunged at his friend and threw him to the floor of the blockhouse, where they engaged in a friendly wrestling match.

It helped to relieve the tension of waiting for attack. Jason, feeling himself a seasoned fighter by this time, was surprised to find that he could still throb with excitement at the prospect of an attack.

There were five days to wait. The waiting was the hardest. The garrison waited, not only for the attack, but especially for reinforcements from Harrison's headquarters at Seneca Town. There were always several men anxiously watching the Sandusky Road on which those reinforcements would come.

Suddenly, on the afternoon of the twenty-fifth, it started. Shots, yells, more shots. The men surged uneasily from one side of the fort to the other.

"That came from the Sandusky Road!"

"They've attacked the fellers comin' to relieve us!"

"Let's go out and help 'em!"

"Sounds like all the Injuns in creation out there!"

Even some of the officers were worried. But when Andy came running toward his three friends, he wore a grin of delight. "I was talkin' to the gen'l's waiter," he said. "An' *he* says that Cap'n McCune just got in from Harrison's headquarters."

"And we got reinforcements comin'?" Abner demanded.

"Not yet."

"Not yet!" All three echoed him, surprised at his cheerful air.

"The cap'n says he had a turr'ble time squirmin' through all them Injuns out there, but all this yellin' and shoutin' and shootin' don't make sense, 'cause the Injuns ain't got anybody to attack!"

Eph was silent a moment, digesting this. "Tryin' to fool us and make us come out," he said finally. "That would be an Injun trick. I doubt Proctor'd have the brains to think of somethin' like that. It must ha' been Tecumseh."

The loud explosion of their own cannon made them jump. "Mebbe they *ain't* foolin'!" Abner cried, but Eph was no longer worried.

Some time later a heavy downpour of rain brought silence. The garrison was still alert, however. And now the spies, sent out to reconnoiter, began to bring word that there had been no battle, after all. The whole thing had been a sham, in an effort to lure the men of the fort outside where they could be annihilated. There was every evidence of a withdrawal of the British forces to their ships.

"We're headin' for Harrison's headquarters."

Dineen came striding over to the hospital the next day. "Where's young Jason?" he called out. When Jason appeared, bearing a basin and a handful of bloodied rags, he smiled. "Want a breath of air?" he asked.

Jason stopped short, understanding him at once. "Where we goin'?" he asked.

Dineen said, in a low voice, as if he did not want others to hear him, "We're headin' for Harrison's head-quarters. Gen'l Clay wants him to know that the Injun force ain't goin' in the British boats, but is headin' over-land to Fort Stephenson."

"I see," Jason said slowly. "The British will come on the fort by water, and the Injuns by land. It ain't a very big fort, neither, is it?"

"Not much bigger'n a buckeye," Dineen said. "But young Croghan is in command, so that makes a differ-ence."

"Wait till I tell the doctor I'm leavin' for a while," Jason said. "And I'll want to tell Eph."

"Meet you at the gate soon as it's dark," Dineen said, and walked away.

There was no talk between them that night. They did not use the road, but kept to one side of it. Twice they skirted large campgrounds of the Indians, skulking silently from tree to tree and bush to bush, their mocca-sins silent upon the earth, their footfalls gentle.

When Jason had counted hundreds of Indians, he felt they might be past the greater number of them, and he said in a low voice, "I'm goin' onto the road. It'll be faster."

"Too dangerous," Dineen said. "I doubt we've passed the last of the critters."

But Jason was sure. "I'll keep to the edge," he said. "Then I kin dodge into the woods any time."

" 'Any time' may be too late," Dineen said drily.

Jason stayed with him, unwilling to go against the decision of a man as wise in the ways of the Indians as Dineen. But as the miles sped by under their long woodsmen's strides, and no other Indians were seen, he was tempted to remark on it.

It was as well he didn't. Dineen stopped abruptly, and moved to one side with a catlike tread. Jason followed suit. He could see nothing, but his nose told him there were Indians nearby. There was the faint, acrid odor of a dying fire, there was the ammoniac smell of horses, there was the strong, somewhat greasy odor of unwashed flesh.

But there was nothing to be seen.

Dineen moved forward like a wraith, Jason following. When Dineen veered to the right, he veered also. And then he saw why. The ranger had almost stepped on a sleeping form. Jason's scalp prickled. Now he could see other forms some distance off, at least twenty of them, humped in slumber and looking like so many rocks. The fire had died completely, but the reek of it was still in the air.

Jason stepped backwards and a twig crackled under his foot. The sleeping Indian roused, and as he sat up, Jason moved to hide behind a tree. The Indian, sleepy as he was, saw the movement, and sprang to his feet with a grunt. He leaped upon Jason like an unwound spring and bore him to the ground.

Every ounce of energy that Jason possessed went into his arms and hands in an effort to break the hold of the attacker, but he might have been trying to squeeze a stone. He tried to roll over and work free, but the Indian was heavier and stronger, and held him fast. Jason thought, suddenly, Who will search for Lucy if I die?

The stone became flesh under his hands as the Indian sagged against him. A powerful arm jerked him to his feet, thrust him ahead. The whole thing had taken less than ten seconds. Jason was dazed. His body felt bruised, his throat sore. His breath came hard, and he struggled to keep it silent. Instinct kept his feet to the familiar pattern of discretion and, his eyes fixed on the retreating form of Dineen, he traveled for half an hour before he felt like himself again.

Then they stopped for a breather. He said, in a low voice, "What happened back there? Did you kill him?"

"Used a knife," Dineen said. "It's quiet." He patted Jason on the back, and before the boy could utter his thanks, he added, "Well, we're even."

CHAPTER 12

THAT was the last encampment they passed. But when morning came they heard horses on the road, and the first band of Indians came into sight. Jason and Dineen were lying flattened behind some brush, motionless.

Several times that morning they had to take to hiding. After the third Indian group had passed by, Dineen went deeper into the forest. They stopped when the sun was high to eat a little, then pushed on again.

General Harrison was at Fort Seneca, and Dineen was passed in to him at once. He was closeted with the general for what seemed a long time to Jason, waiting outside the house. He braced his back against the wall and rested his tired legs upon the ground.

Dineen was a fine man to work with. Jason knew he would never again question the older man's reasons for caution. Not after last night's experience, he thought with a grin. He flexed his arms and hands. They seemed strong, yet how helpless they had been against that Indian.

When Dineen came out, he said quietly, "Goin' to git on to Fort Stephenson, lad. Want to come?"

Jason was on his feet with a bound. "How far is it?"

"Just a hop and a holler," Dineen said. "Likely eight-ten miles. Not fur enough to limber up your knee joints."

For answer, Jason swung into step beside him. "Nice little fort they're makin' here," he said conversationally.

"More like a fortified camp," Dineen said.

"Aye. The gen'l has more'n a thousand men here he kin send out in any direction where they're needed, they tell me. Most of 'em are reg'lars."

"You kin have 'em," Dineen snorted. "They're pretty good in a fight, and I'd be the last to deny our militia has backed down as often as they've gone forrard, but when it comes to fightin' in the woods, I'll do without the reg'lars."

This was a long speech from Dineen, and Jason knew that meant his friend was deeply stirred. "How many they got at Fort Stephenson?" he asked.

"Hunnerd and sixty."

Jason was aghast. "Hunnerd and sixty!" he cried, thinking of the thousands who had come to besiege Fort Meigs, and who were now on their way to attack the little fort. "Why—that's nothin'!"

"I told you before, they got Croghan in command. He's as good as a couple hunnerd himself."

The miles sped by, and they were soon cautiously approaching Fort Stephenson. To their right the Sandusky

River made a small curve. Dineen pointed to the land beyond. "Good high spot for the Injuns," he remarked tersely.

The fort was humming with activity. Small as it was, Jason thought it was well laid out, with the pickets properly banked, a good dry ditch beyond the wall, and a glacis beyond that. Troops would not easily storm this little fort.

He was surprised to note that Dineen did not head at once for Major Croghan's headquarters. Instead, he stopped to talk to several men he knew slightly. When he saw Jason's questioning eyes upon him, he turned with a grin. "I ain't carryin' dispatches, lad," he said.

"Didn't Gen'l Harrison send word by you?" Jason asked.

"Nay, he asked me a mort o' questions, and then he was goin' to call a lot of his officers for a powwow. Likely they won't send word of what they decide until tonight some time."

"Then why—" Jason began.

"Why'd I come on here? The fun's goin' to start soon, and I wanted to be here when it began," Dineen answered.

Jason discovered that the hospital was a small building to the right of the gate and near the military storehouses. He went to volunteer his services, for he well knew that if the attack came in force there would be need of him there. He soon got into conversation with the doctor, and gave him news of the sick and wounded at Fort Meigs.

"We lost more'n a tenth of our men there," Jason told him, "from camp fever. The Injuns didn't git anywhere near that many. Exceptin' for Colonel Dudley's men," he added, anxious to stick to the truth. "But they never rightly were *in t*he fort."

The doctor nodded. "Men inveigh against war," he said with a thoughtful air, "yet they accept death's hand in disease without a murmur. I have known whole territories to be roused by the slaughter of one family by the redskins, yet there was no public protest at the loss of dozens of their children by putrid sore throat. . . . Someday we shall turn from the conquest of nations to the conquest of disease."

After having been so long in a fort so large that it encompassed fourteen acres, was staffed by more than a thousand men, and defended by batteries of cannon and mortars, Jason found little Fort Stephenson a welcome relief. The men knew one another; the commander knew them all. There was no problem to find crews for the artillery, for it consisted of one small six-pounder which the men had named Good Bess in affection.

Jason found plenty to do. Dineen was soon exchanging news with some former cronies, and helping in the readying of the fort against attack. They all knew that an attack was coming, and they did not have much time to prepare for it. Despite the smallness of the fort, and the size of the attacking party, Jason found the men distinctly cheerful. Well, he thought, there was this to say for the regulars—their business was fighting.

The following morning, toward noon, a messenger arrived from Harrison. He was worn and wearied, for he had been sent out the night before, about midnight, and had lost his way in the dark, so that he was hours late in arriving.

In the mysterious fashion of the army grapevine, the soldiers knew what was in his dispatch almost as soon as Major Croghan did. And they could not have been more indignant.

"They'd be fools to do it!" Dineen said explosively. Jason had never seen him so angry.

"Do what?"

"Harrison has ordered Croghan and his men to retreat to Fort Seneca. Why, it would be another massacre like the one at Fort Dearborn! That messenger says the forest is swarmin' with Injuns, and I kin well believe it. You know how many we passed on our way. They've all got here by this time, and plenty more besides. What on earth was the gen'l thinkin' of, anyhow?"

"Mebbe he thinks this place couldn't last against the British cannon," Jason offered.

Croghan called a conference of his officers, and in a very short time had sent the messenger back to Harrison. Word of his decision leaked out just as fast as the previous news had, and men went about grinning to one another, and slapping their thighs with glee. "Know what he said? He said, 'We have determined to maintain this place, and by heavens we can.' That's what he said!"

It was easy to understand why Croghan was beloved by his men.

This was not the end of the matter, however. That same day Colonel Ball and his corps of dragoons arrived at the fort, bringing Colonel Wells and a message from Harrison. The message ordered Croghan back to Fort Seneca, and gave the command of Fort Stephenson to Colonel Wells.

The men were astounded. "That's what he gits for savin' our scalps," one of them grumbled to Jason. "Now he'll likely git cashiered for bein' a sensible man as well as a brave one. Why, did you know these fellers were attacked by Injuns on their way here? Left seventeen of 'em for dead, they say."

Colonel Ball and his dragoons departed once more, taking Major Croghan with them, and the men were angry. Dineen shook his head. "I doubt Gen'l Harrison heard the right of it. But mebbe the major kin set him straight."

Major Croghan did plead his cause so well that Harrison sent him back the following day, and returned the command of the fort to him. Now things began to hum. Everything was being readied for attack, and when a reconnoitering party returned from Sandusky Bay to say that they had seen Proctor's gunboats approaching, there was little to do but wait for them. To get in practice, the men fired their little six-pounder at some of the Indians across the river, and laughed to see them scatter.

"Good Bess took a broom to 'em that time!" Dineen laughed.

That afternoon the gunboats hove into sight. Good Bess spoke again and again, but to little effect. They anchored in a little cove half a mile from the fort and landed a howitzer. The Indians deployed to the flanks and rear of the fort to cut off any possible retreat. Then two British officers appeared with a flag of truce.

"Seems like they'd ruther talk than fight," growled Dineen. "What they waitin' for?"

Lieutenant Shipp was sent out to talk with the British, and the men, lining the palisades, could see that he was refusing some offer. Just as he turned to go back into the fort, an Indian sprang from a bushy ravine and tried to snatch his sword. Shipp would have killed the savage if one of the British officers had not saved him.

Major Croghan was furious at this violation of the truce, and called out to his lieutenant, "Shipp, come in, and we will blow them all to hell!" Almost at once the firing began from the gunboats.

All night long the British cannon roared. They did little damage to the fort, however, and the Americans answered every now and then with Good Bess, moving her from one blockhouse to another, to make the enemy think they had several guns.

Unfortunately, there was little ammunition for the six-pounder, and the commander was not willing to waste it shooting at targets in the dark. After a while Good Bess was silent, and then she was moved to the blockhouse in the middle of the north side of the fort. If an assault came, it would probably be at the northwest corner, for that was the weakest place in the fort. And with the cannon so placed, it could rake the ditch at the northwest angle. Once Good Bess was in place, she was masked so that she would not be spied until the Americans were ready to use her.

Daylight disclosed that the British had dragged three of their guns to a high point—higher than the fort itself —and now these opened fire. The Americans did not reply, and as the day wore on, and there was no answering fire, Proctor grew impatient.

"He's got to do somethin' soon," Dineen said to Jason. "Don't fergit he's got Injuns, and they don't take kindly to sittin' idle when a fight's been promised. He'll start the attack before long."

It was obvious that Major Croghan thought so, too. Bags of sand, and even bags of flour, were piled against the pickets of the weak northwest angle. At the same time, Proctor's cannonading grew stronger upon that same point. When a thunderstorm began to rumble in the distance, the assault began.

Under cover of the heavy smoke from the cannonading, the storming party got within twenty paces of the
fort before they were seen. Kentucky sharpshooters, at

their posts within the fort, then let their rifles bark. "I
got the feller on the end!" "Look at his hat fly off!" "I'm
goin' to git me an officer!" the men yelled.

There was momentary confusion in the British line,

but then the redcoats rallied. Men with axes raced over
the glacis, jumped into the ditch, and began to chop at
the pickets. Their leader was a lieutenant colonel who
shouted that they should "show the Yankees no
quarter."

Now, when the ditch was full of men, Good Bess
was unmasked and spoke with terrible emphasis. Slugs
and grapeshot ripped through the mass of human flesh
crowded into the ditch, leaving it strewn with bodies.

The British tried once more, but again the rifles and
Good Bess took their toll, and this time there was a
frantic retreat. A corps of British grenadiers, arriving at
the south side of the fort at this time, received a dis-
couraging hail of rifle bullets, and raced back to the forest for safety.

"Didn't see many Injuns, did you, lad?" Dineen
asked, wiping the barrel of his rifle with a cloth. "They
don't like fightin' in the open. Never did."

But Jason did not reply. He was on his way to the
hospital where the doctor greeted him with a grin. "Not
a very expensive attack for us, was it?" he said jovially.
"All we've got is one dead, and seven wounded. I call
that a record."

There were plenty of wounded lying outside the fort,
however. Their cries rose piteously upon the Sabbath
air. When night came, Croghan ordered buckets of
water to be lowered to the sufferers outside the pickets,
and a small trench was dug, which communicated with

the ditch, and in this way many of the wounded were carried into the fort.

The doctor sent for Jason. "Now we do have our work cut out for us," he said. "But, thank God, these are the enemy, and not our own men."

CHAPTER 13

"So this is Canady!" one of the soldiers exclaimed as he set foot on Canadian soil at Amherstburg.

"Don't look any different from Ohio," Abner commented. "Though Ohio ain't so smoky." The other laughed appreciatively. Proctor, in retreating from Fort Malden, had set the storehouses afire, and the smoke hung low in the air.

"Where are all them brave Canadian soldiers?" Andy demanded. "I don't see any. Only some women over there, cryin' and talkin' to the officers. What they cryin' for?"

"They're afeared of us, I reckon," Eph said.

"Afeared of us? What for? We don't fight women!" Abner cried indignantly.

"No, nor we don't let our Injun allies scalp our prisoners. But the Britishers do, and they're afeared we'll do likewise."

Jason left them talking and went forward to where Dineen was standing at ease, one hand on his hip, the other holding his long rifle.

"Glad to see you, Jason," he said. "We might mebbe have a job to do."

Ever since Jason and Dineen had been together during the siege of Fort Stephenson, the older man had treated him like an equal. Jason's shoulders were broad enough now for a man's, and he was taller than Eph. His face was as serious as a man's, too, for Lucy's capture had aged him.

"Where to?" he asked.

"Dunno. But we may git sent ahead of the troops to spy against the British. Or mebbe we'll git sent to Detroit. They're talkin' about it now." He jerked his head to where a knot of officers surrounded General Harrison's lean figure.

When one of them beckoned him, he moved with less of a slouch than usual. Jason saw him receive his orders, saw him sketch a salute, and return. By the time he reached Jason, he was grinning broadly.

"You'll never light on what they want us to do!" he said, shaking his head in wonderment.

"Bring back Proctor as a prisoner?"

"Nope. That might be easier, at that!"

"Well, what?"

"They want us to round up some hosses. They went and left their own hosses back in Ohio."

"There wasn't room for the horses on the boats," Jason said. The army had been ferried to Canada in Perry's victorious fleet.

"Sure there wasn't. But they thought they'd find plenty here. And so far they haven't found a one!"

There were others detailed to hunt for horses, yet though they searched every barn and outbuilding, and combed the fields and the woods, they found no horses. Dineen managed to corner one small pony, and this he led proudly to headquarters.

Governor Shelby of Kentucky, who had brought five thousand volunteers to Harrison for this invasion of Canada, was elderly, so he was given the pony. The others walked.

They reached Sandwich at the same time that Colonel Johnson and his regiment of mounted riflemen reached Detroit, across the river. They had traveled overland while the main body of the army went in Perry's ships. Detroit was already in American hands again, for General McArthur had crossed over with seven hundred men, had driven off the Indians surrounding the town, and taken it again. The happy residents of Detroit had run up the American flag even before the troops landed.

Now Harrison sent word for Johnson and his men to cross to Canada at once, for he was determined to pursue Proctor and his army as quickly as possible, and cavalry would be of wonderful assistance.

Eph and Jason stood watching the boats unload the Kentucky men and their horses. It was the evening of October first. Eph was already yawning. "I'm goin' to git me some sleep pretty soon," he said to his brother. "We'll be marchin' in the mornin' early, I'll bet. And if we catch up with Proctor and Tecumseh tomorrow, I want to be feelin' fresh and spry."

Jason was not listening. He was leaning forward, peering at one of the disembarking men. "It looks like . . ." he muttered. Then, suddenly, he let out a shout, "It is!" and raced away.

"Is what?" Eph asked the empty air before he sped after his brother.

But he knew what it was soon as he saw Jason talking to the man. Jason was pointing excitedly to the belt of wampum which the Kentuckian wore. His questions streamed out so fast the man had no chance to answer.

"Where'd you git it? Did you see her? Was she all right? How'd you happen to find her?"

The man was tall and bearded. He shook his head in dismay. "Slow down a minute, son," he remonstrated. "Yore tongue is goin' to be so fur ahead of yore body, you'll never catch up. Be dumb the rest of yore born days, I wouldn't wonder."

Jason paused for breath. "The wampum," he said then, trying hard to sound sensible. "Where'd you git it?"

"Bought it off'n an Injun in Dee-troit," the man said.

Jason's face fell. "You didn't see a white girl—about so high—with the Injun, did you?"

"N-no," the man said slowly, "but the Injun did say this was a very valuable piece of wampum, and he'd got it off'n a Wyandot chief."

Jason bit his lip. To be so close to learning Lucy's whereabouts, and to be so baffled! He lowered his eyes, unwilling to have the Kentuckian see the hurt in them.

"But," the man added softly, "he *did* say that this here chief had three childern, and one of 'em was white."

Jason's eyes flew up to search the man's face. Was he telling the truth, or only trying to make him feel better? It was the truth, surely! "Where—where is this chief? Did he say?"

"Nope. Only said he was with Tecumseh."

"Tecumseh. Then—mebbe he's here—in Canada."

"That's what I'd think." The man looked across at Eph. "Friend of yores?"

"A good friend," Eph said. "Jason, we must tell the major."

Major Vernon, when he heard the news, could hardly wait for the army to advance. He fretted, in a low voice, "But if the Indians run—and they often do from artillery and ordered battle—they'll take her with them. Or she may be exposed to the fire of the armies. If only we knew which chief, and where he is!"

The regiment to which Eph and Abner and Andy Frazier were attached was to be left behind to garrison Sandwich. Dineen was to act as spy in advance of the troops, and Jason went with him as a matter of course. When Eph protested that he would desert if he had to stay behind while the others went after Proctor, Dineen asked for him, too, and Eph was hurriedly transferred to the rangers.

The army marched at good speed along the road that bordered the waters of Lake St. Clair, and there they came upon seven British deserters. Dineen led them back to headquarters, and the men were questioned. Yes, they said, Proctor was encamped fifteen miles up the Thames River. Yes, he had at least seven hundred British troops, and about twelve hundred Indians under Tecumseh.

Dineen, returning to his friends that evening, told them what the men had related. "Fust off," he said, "I'm bettin' a sharpshin to a bearskin that Tecumseh is wishin' he didn't have Proctor for an ally."

Eph said, "Can't say I blame him."

"You know what that Britisher did?" Dineen continued. "He told Tecumseh there was a naval battle out on the lake last month, when Perry won his victory. He had to, 'cause anybody could hear the sound o' the guns. *But* he never told him that the British had lost their hull fleet. They say Tecumseh paddled out—far out—on the lake, listenin' to the cannon. When the British fleet didn't come back, Proctor told him they had won, but the Injuns knew better."

The pursuit of Proctor grew hotter the following day. The sloops which had been able to follow the troops by water, carrying supplies and covering the men as they crossed the river, were no longer able to do so. The current became swift and turbulent. The flat banks had grown high and dangerous. It was too easy for Indian snipers to pick off the men on board, and almost impossible for the Americans to retaliate.

Proctor fled from Doulsen's farm, where he had been encamped, to Chatham, where he seemed prepared to make a stand. Indians were posted at two bridges across the wild waters of McGregor's Creek, but the American artillery scattered them at one, and a charge of the Kentucky cavalry dispersed them at the other.

Just as the bridges had been repaired, and the Americans were about to advance, a Wyandot chieftain, with sixty warriors in his train, came to Harrison.

"What's he want? Is he surrenderin'?" Eph asked Dineen.

"Dunno. I think he want to join us. He was with Proctor before. This chief's a big man with the Wyandots. His name's Walk-in-the-Water."

Jason had heard only part of this. "Did you say Wyandot?" he cried. "Mebbe he knows where Lucy is." Without waiting for an answer he dashed off to where the Indians stood.

Dineen came with him. "I kin talk their language," he said. "Let me ask."

Jason could scarcely wait for the lengthy conversation to end. Dineen spoke first to one, and then another of the Indians. They were about to leave for the Detroit

River, well behind the lines, and there was not much time. But the talk was unhurried.

When he came back to where Jason and Eph were waiting, Dineen was smiling. "Found out a little, anyhow," he said. "And I think it's good."

"Do they know her? Did they know where she is?"

"They know her all right. I was talkin' to the man who took her into his family. He says she was a spunky little thing. Not in those words, exactly . . ."

"Yes, yes," Jason cried. "But where is she now?"

"He says he don't know. Two days ago she disappeared. And her horse, too."

"Diana?"

"Diana. He described her all right. They'd have gone lookin' for her, if they hadn't been on the move with Proctor. No time to hunt for a lost daughter."

"Daughter! Had he adopted her?"

"Not yet, but he was goin' to, he said."

Jason was silent. If Lucy had escaped on Diana, she might be somewhere near. Or she might have circled away from the armies and be back at Malden, or Sandwich, or even Detroit by this time. But at least she was alive. "Spunky." Yes, she had courage.

Jason, Eph, and Dineen were among the first over the bridge. Their duty was to range ahead of the troops, flushing any Indians who might have taken cover for purposes of sniping, locating the enemy, and estimating his numbers. There were many spies out, and the reports they brought in were encouraging. Proctor's army appeared to be in full retreat. The Americans began to wonder if the British would ever stand and fight.

"Tecumseh will see to it," Eph said. "He is not one to turn tail like that Proctor." But the Americans captured two gunboats, several prisoners, and bateaux with army supplies, without any sign of the British army.

There were rapids in the Thames River at Arnold's Mill, but the Americans got across by means of Colonel Johnson's horses. Each of the mounted riflemen took one of the infantry soldiers on his horse behind him, and soon the entire army was on the north side of the river.

Jason stood watching the maneuver. He had been sent back to the lines with a message from Dineen and, having delivered it, he paused to watch the orderly advance across the swift water. Suddenly he moved forward, just as one of the soldiers jumped down from the horse which had ferried him across.

"Aren't you Thomas Brinkley?" he asked. His gaze went instinctively to the man's arm.

"Aye, and you're the lad that saved me in the woods." Brinkley's voice was hesitant, though his words were so positive. "Robert Potter's brother, I remember."

Jason nodded. "You healed up well," he said, pleased that his doctoring had been so successful.

The man was fumbling in a pouch hanging from his belt. "Here, I want you to have this," he said. He took

Jason's hand, and pressed some money into it, then closed the fingers around it. "Give it to your brother," he said. "I've a feelin' I'll not come back this time."

Jason felt a little shiver go down his back. "You'll come through it," he said with assumed heartiness. "It begins to look like we wouldn't even git to fight the Britishers—they're runnin' so fast."

"Oh, we'll fight 'em, all right," Brinkley said with a mournful shake of his head. "This day or the next. And I'll not come out of it, neither."

Jason had to run to get back to Eph and Dineen. He knew that they had gone ahead and that they were to bear north of the river. With every sense alert for the enemy, he still found a part of his brain marveling at the change in Brinkley. Perhaps the man did have a premonition of death. He did not see how anything else could have wrought such a change in him.

Perhaps because he was so absorbed in the mystery of Brinkley, he missed the place where Eph and Dineen had turned off, and had to retrace his steps. His eyes searched the ground, flicked across the woodland, up at the trees.

Something brown was moving in the woods not twenty yards away! Moving stealthily and quietly. He froze where he was, thankful that he was half-concealed by underbrush. Slowly, he began to sink from sight, his hand gripping his rifle, and bringing it to the ready.

The distant figure paused also, as if aware it had been seen. Then, suddenly, it began to run toward him.

"Jason! Jason Potter!" came in a high happy voice.

Jason covered the ground between them in great leaps, and caught Lucy in a bear hug. "You're safe!" he cried. "You're alive!"

She giggled a little, half in merriment, half in nervous relief. "I won't be for long, if you squeeze the breath out of me," she protested.

He held her out at arm's length, studying her. Her soft, light brown curls were gone, and her hair was parted and worn in two short braids. It looked as if it had not been combed for several days. Her face and arms and legs were brown and scratched. She wore an old gray blanket, belted with a piece of untanned deerskin.

But her eyes were clear, and her smile was as sweet as ever. "If you only knew how we worried," he said.

"And I," she told him. "I have never ceased wondering if my father was killed that terrible day. Does he still live?" she asked, seeing Jason's smile.

"The bullet tore a furrow in his scalp. He was only half-concious for several days. But he's well now, and here with the army."

"Then there *is* an invasion!" she cried. "Oh, how I have longed for news! The little I heard made small sense to me."

He dismissed the events of the past few months with

"You're safe!" he cried. "You're alive!"

a toss of his head. "What *I* want to know is how you got here?"

She laughed. "I got here by doing all the things you taught me, Jason. There was no use escaping until now, when there were rumors that the American army was coming. Where would I have gone? How would I have lived? But when I heard the news, I went at night and loosed Diana—for I did not want her to remain a prisoner if I went free—and then I went off into the woods."

"You didn't ride her?" he asked.

"I couldn't mount her. There was no saddle. I have been living in the woods for two days now. But oh, Jason, I do *not* like the taste of bulrushes!"

Jason laughed, too. "But you're alive, ain't you? That's the important thing. Just wait till your pa sees you! He'll be givin' a medal to the bulrushes."

He took her to the rear, and soon they met the advance troops—Colonel Johnson's mounted riflemen. The men stared in amazement at the young white girl in her coarse blanket, and some of them grinned and saluted. The infantry was behind them, and there they found Major Vernon.

Jason could not stay to watch more than the first moment of reunion, but he went back to the van with a broad grin on his face. With Lucy safe, he knew that the worst of the war was over for him.

By the time he found Eph and Dineen again, he had also found the British and the Indians. They were drawn up in battle order, and the spies went forward and to the sides to locate the various troops.

It was not long before Colonel Johnson's mounted riflemen took their position in the van—only the spies being between them and the enemy. Dineen looked questioningly at Eph. "Never heard of such a thing," he said. "They goin' to start with a charge?"

"Looks like it," Eph said. "I never heard of it, neither."

A bugle blew, and the American line began to advance. Slowly, because of the great trees, some of which lay fallen on the ground, and the dense undergrowth. As they neared the British front, they were fired upon— not once, but twice. Horses reared and screamed, some went down, some tried to run back toward the rear. But the Kentuckians soon had them in hand again, and with a yell of *"Remember the Raisin!"* they raced upon the British.

The enemy broke under the charge, which continued at full speed toward the second British line. Again they broke, and when the Kentuckians had dashed through, they wheeled about and rode upon the British from the rear, firing as they came.

Jason and Eph, watching the battle, stood open-mouthed. In five minutes that section of it was over.

The British soldiers threw down their arms and begged for mercy.

Suddenly Dineen cried, "There goes Proctor!" and he began to run.

Jason ran after him, calling, "He's got a horse and carriage! You can't make it!"

Nor did he. Some of the Kentucky riflemen turned their horses in pursuit of the vanishing general, but Dineen, unheeding for the first time in his life, failed to see the Indian sniper.

Jason heard the report, and took aim in an instant. But he did not wait to see if his shot had taken effect. He was kneeling beside his friend, exploring with fearful fingers the hole in his thigh.

Dineen grunted. "No fool like an old fool," he muttered. "After watchin' every grass blade for all these months, I had to go and lose my head over that old Proctor. Didn't even *see* that bullet comin' at me!"

Jason supported him to the rear, after he had stanched the flow of blood. There were still sounds of battle off to the left, where the greater number of the Indians were ranged beyond a large swamp. Half of Colonel Johnson's men had gone that way, under the doughty colonel himself. They met him being led from the field on a white pony, and when Dineen saw him he straightened a little.

"I ain't so bad off," he said. "Look at the colonel there. He's really shot up."

The pony was, too, for it dropped dead as they reached the surgeon's battle station.

"Wonder where Eph is," Jason said.

"Ain't seen him since right after the charge," Dineen answered. "Likely in the woods, lookin' for a fight."

Jason would have stayed to help at the station if he had not been worried about Eph. There had been at least one sniper, as Dineen's wounded thigh bore witness. There might well have been two or more. He knew that Eph was cautious, but he was worried about him nevertheless. The sounds of shooting from the left were faint and sporadic now. The battle was really over.

He left Dineen resting comfortably in a wagon, and went back to where he and Eph had parted. The river was on the right, a swamp on the left. The dead and wounded lay on the ground between.

For the first, and perhaps the last, time in his life Jason ignored the injured, promising himself that he would soon return. He walked into the swampy region, his eyes searching for his brother.

Eph came toward him unexpectedly, appearing from behind a dense growth, and leading a horse. The poor beast was frightened, and its eyes were rolling. The once satiny coat was long and scarred, but the telltale crescent marking could still be seen on its forehead.

"Diana!" Jason cried. "Where'd you find her?"

"Saw her in the distance and went after her. I'd know

her anywhere, I guess." Eph's laugh was rare, but he laughed now. "Well," he said, "we've got the Vernon family reunited. And we've got the British licked. I reckon we kin go home now."

CHAPTER 14

Jason wished that he could have seen the reunion between Lucy and her mare, but there were the wounded to attend to. As he searched the battlefield, he kept looking for Brinkley, who had been so sure he was going to die this day. He was not among the dead, nor did Jason find him moaning on the field or at the battle station toward the rear. He combed the small swamp, but did not have time to investigate the large swamp where the Kentuckians had fought so bravely, dismounting from their horses in order to move more freely. That was where Tecumseh had led his Indians in their last stand.

Someone said that Tecumseh had died in that furious fight; someone else said that it was he who had first wounded Colonel Johnson, and that Johnson had drawn his pistol and killed the Indian warrior. But although Jason saw many Indians who had been killed, none of them suited his mental picture of the Indian leader.

He worked hard for the rest of the afternoon, doing whatever he could do to assist the surgeons. They were glad of his help, for by this time Jason's name and abilities were known to several of them, and his deft handling of the wounded was more than welcome.

He was tired when he found the lean-to which Eph had made. "Wish Abner was here," Eph said, making a small fire to cook their rations. "And Andy, too, o' course."

"And James Dineen," Jason added. "Wonder if they got him onto one of the boats goin' downstream."

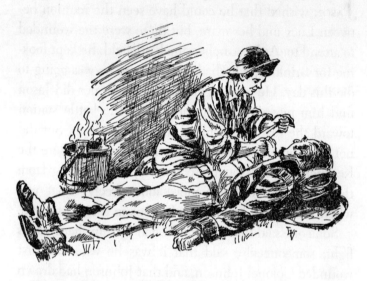

"I wouldn't wonder," Eph said. A figure loomed above them and Jason looked up, half-expecting to see Dineen, he had been thinking of him so hard.

It was Brinkley. "That money I gave you for safe-keepin'," he said to Jason. "I'd like it back now." He said it as if he meant it.

Jason's mouth fell open. "You gave me the money to repay my brother Robert," he said. "And Robert shall have it," he added, rising to his feet and staring hard at Brinkley.

Brinkley took a threatening step toward him. "Give it back, I say!" His thin lips snarled.

Jason had never known a man could lie so convincingly, and he was furious. "It's time you learned to pay your just debts," he cried. "But since you need help in doin' it, I'll oblige. By handin' the money to Robert, and no one else! You were willin' enough to let him have it this noon when you thought you were goin' to die in battle."

"I said no such thing!" But the belligerent voice was fading into a whine.

Eph rose slowly to his feet. "You callin' my brother a liar?" he asked in a deceptively mild voice.

For answer the man swore, and stumbled off into the night. Eph turned to stare at Jason. "Well," he said with a chuckle, "Robert is sure goin' to be surprised when you give him that money. How much is it?"

"I don't know," Jason said, relaxing with a smile. "I never counted it. I was too busy."

By the following week the army was back in Sandwich. There was a happy meeting with Abner and Andy, not even marred by the storm of snow and wind which had swept in from the lake. Eph and Jason found that their friends were snugly settled in a lean-to which kept out most of the weather. Andy had a fire going, and was roasting a fat fowl in celebration.

"Where'd you git it?" Jason asked. "You didn't shoot *that* in the woods!"

"Well," Andy said carefully, "you might say I sort o' bought it."

Abner burst into laughter. "With threats and bribes," he said. "That's how he 'bought' it!"

Andy pursed his lips with an air of consideration. "I wouldn't call it that. I told this poor woman that had a lot o' hens they weren't safe with a lot o' hungry American soldiers around. And she got scairt and said if I'd pertect 'em, she'd give me one. So I did, and she did."

"How'd you pertect 'em? That's what you ain't told," Abner prodded him.

Andy's grin was a trifle shamefaced. "I just happened to mention to some of the fellers that there were a lot o' females needed pertection in this woman's house, so they started paradin' back and forth in front of it. How'd I know the old woman would think they had an eye on her hens? And how'd I know the fellers thought I meant women when I said 'females'?"

That hen was the tastiest meat they had had in weeks, and when the last of the tender bones had been crunched and sucked dry, and the fire had died down, they prepared to lie down for the night. Jason was hunting a dry corner when the blanket which served as a door to the lean-to was pulled aside.

"Is this where— Ah, there you are, Jason!" Major Vernon held the blanket up so that Lucy could enter, and then followed her. The men got to their feet, but the lean-to was so low that only Lucy could stand upright in it.

She looked like the old Lucy again, Jason thought, her hair framing her face with curls. Most of the scratches had healed, and she was dressed in a woolen gown with a pelisse to cover it against the weather. Only the tan color of her face remained to remind one of her captivity.

"Sit down, men," the major said. "Do you mind if we join you? I have not had the chance to thank either of you," he nodded toward Eph and Jason as he spoke, "for all you did. But you may rest assured I am the most grateful man in the world. To have my daughter back, whole and healthy, and to know that if it had not been for your teaching, Jason—" His voice broke a little, and he paused to master it.

"I shall have to devote years of my life to teaching Jason Latin and Greek in order to make up for it," Lucy said with a smile. "Not that I know any Greek! And he'll probably find it as distasteful as I found the bulrushes."

Now that the first embarrassing moments were over, the men spread a blanket on the ground for Lucy and her father, and they sat down around the fire.

"I had to come tonight," the major said, "because I have just learned that I am to be transferred to the Niagara front. This time I shall *not* let Lucy persuade me to take her along. She shall go back to Cincinnati where she will be cared for properly."

Abner said, "Didn't do her any real harm, Major Vernon. I think the little lady could take most anythin' in her stride, though she did have us all worried white-haired."

Lucy said, "Some of it wasn't at all pleasant, but I'm glad it happened, in a way. It taught me so many things."

"Such as how to eat bulrushes?" her father asked with a fond smile.

She did not smile in reply, but said seriously, "At first, when they took my clothes from me and gave them to a little Indian girl, I wept. But I soon learned that clothes are not worth weeping for. There were so many other things I really cared about—my father's safety, and my friends'." She beamed at all of them around the little fire. "Most of all, my country. I wanted so for us to win. When I saw—some of the things I saw"—she paled a little at the memory—"I realized that, with all its faults, our country deserves to win. Must win!"

It was an intense little speech, and they were silenced by it for a while. Then Eph said gently, "It may take another year or two to lick the British in other directions, but they're finished here in the Northwest. And once these years of fightin' are over, I think they'll prove to the world that we are a nation to reckon with!"

Major Vernon said, "That's something I hope for. Too many of the world's people still think of us as a sort of appendage of Great Britain—not her colonies any more, but something not too far removed from it. And we *are* a nation—young, admittedly, but growing stronger all the time."

"And larger," Abner said with a wry smile. "I know, 'cause I've walked over enough of it to wear my feet down to the shinbones."

They all laughed. Jason wished that he could say something wise and important, for he felt that this was, in spite of the laughter, a solemn moment. Lucy and the major stood up to go, and he had still not thought of anything to say.

Lucy took his hand in hers. "Do you remember what I said to you when Father and I left Fort Meigs?" she asked.

"You said, 'I'll be back,'" he told her, for he had never forgotten.

"I kept my word, didn't I?" she smiled up at him. "Now I want you to say something to me."

He swallowed hard. "What is it?"

"I want you to tell me that you will study hard to become a doctor," she said. "Even if it means studying things you don't want to study."

"Latin and Greek, too?"

"Latin and Greek, too."

"All right," he said, "I will."

It was a promise.

GLOSSARY

glacis	an embankment of earth, sloping up to a fortification, so that attackers would be exposed to the gunfire of the defenders
pelisse	a long cloak or outer coat
putrid sore throat	it was not until 1819 that this was known as diphtheria
sharp shin	a piece of cut money
spies	men who scouted for the army. Always good woodsmen, they sometimes penetrated the enemy lines, or mingled with the Indian allies of the enemy to get information. Some of them could do this because they had been kidnapped as children and raised by the Indians
traverse	a defensive trench with a wall of earth above
waiter	the personal servant of an officer, an orderly

wampum   the money of the Indians, orig-
inally made of shells, later of beads
that the Indians got from traders.
The old "black wampum" was
made of purple shells, and was
much more valuable than the white
wampum.